SECRET AGENT 6th GRADER 4
SELFIES ARE FOREVER

BY MARCUS EMERSON
AND NOAH CHILD

ILLUSTRATED BY DAVID LEE

EMERSON PUBLISHING HOUSE

This one's for Olivia...

Text copyright © 2013 by Emerson Publishing House.
Illustrations copyright © David Lee

Emerson Publishing House

Book design by Marcus Emerson.

So there I was… holding a water balloon filled with onion-baked beans while a bunch of kids wearing heavy robes watched to see what I was going to do next. My ankles felt weaker with every second that ticked by. Hey, if there was a way to buff up my ankles, I'd sign up in a heartbeat, but there's not, so I can't! Until I make a "6 Minute Ankles" workout video, I'll just have to live with this curse.

"Earth to Brody!" Maddie said, super annoyed. "Get your head back in the game!"

"Yeah, dude!" the *other* Maddie said. "Quit spacing out!"

Oh, right, there was also that –*two* different Maddies were standing in front of me.

If you think *you're* confused, imagine how *I* felt.

I shook my head, looking back and forth between the

two identical blonde haired girls with purple fabric draped across their shoulders.

There were only slight differences between them, like one of them had a small mole on her cheekbone and the other didn't, but I had no idea if the real Maddie had a mole there or not!

"Get on with it, Brody!" Maddie on the right commanded. "Time's running out! Most of the show choir has already taken the stage, and if we don't get out there *now*, then those kids are completely flooped!"

"I know!" my voice cracked, making it obvious that I had no clue what to do.

"Soak her with the beans already!" the Maddie on the right continued.

The Maddie on the left made a face so angry that it scared me. "Don't you dare do it! Soak *her!*" she said, tilting her head at the other girl.

"I swear to the ghost of James Buchanan himself," Maddie on the right said, "If you pitch that balloon of beans at me, you'll regret it for the *rest* of your life."

That kind of sounded like my Maddie.

"Ditto!" Maddie on the left said.

Ugh...

"Will the real Maddie please step forward?" I asked, half-jokingly.

Both of the girls took one step forward, and they both had the exact same "annoyed-to-play-this-game" look on their faces.

I lifted the baked bean balloon, darting my eyes between both of the blonde girls standing in front of me.

"I'm the real Maddie!" Maddie on the left said with a tremble. It almost sounded like she was going to start crying. "Brody, listen to me. It's *me*, *your* Maddie. Remember all the good times we've had? Remember all the funny things we've said to each other?"

"OMG," Maddie on the right said. "Seriously, Brody, *I'm* the real Maddie and this is really starting to get on my nerves! The fact that you can't tell us apart is a little disappointing!"

Finally, I had an idea. I looked at the Maddie on the right, who was clearly more upset than the other girl. "If you're the real Maddie, then tell me – what was the first thing you said to me when we met?"

The girl clenched her fists as her face turned red. "Like I can even remember something like that!" she said through her teeth, and then she turned the question around on me. "What did *you* say to *me* when we first met?"

I sighed, nodding. "Touché."

The Maddie on the left took another step toward me. Her eyes sparkled with what looked like tears. "Brody," she said again, softly. "Please… please don't do this. Don't make a mistake. Okay? We've come so far as friends… please… do the right thing."

"The right thing?" the other Maddie said. "You mean by popping that balloon on *me?*"

The Maddie on the left didn't break eye contact. She took another step in my direction, reaching her hand out for me to take.

I tried to back up, but the kids behind me kept me from moving in that direction. All this trouble simply because I didn't want Glitch to fall apart.

"Please," the Maddie closest to me pleaded again, her eyes twinkling. "Give me that baked bean balloon."

And then, as if the planet screeched to a stop, I knew exactly what I had to do. It was so obvious that I almost felt like a noob…

My name is Brody Valentine, and I'm a secret agent.

That morning was probably one of the best mornings I'd ever had at Buchanan School. The weather was a cool sixty-five degrees with a strong breeze, which just happened to be my favorite weather because it meant students got to wear sweat pants during gym class.

I like that because sweats are totes cozy… and they hide

my skinny ankles.

Classes for the entire first half of the day were void of any kind of assignments. It was just movies and snacks for the sixth graders of Buchanan.

The last half of the day, all the sixth graders were gonna get bussed to the mall to watch the Buchanan School show choir do their thing. The parents of the kids in show choir were also going to attend.

The reason was because our sixth grade show choir had recently won the city championships for having the best performance out of all the other middle schools in the area.

It wasn't exactly a state championship victory like the high schools get, but for us middle schoolers, it was kind of a big deal. Well, to the middle schoolers *in* the show choir, it was. To the rest of the sixth grade class at Buchanan, well, we were just happy to get a half-day. I can totally see why my dad gets stoked about half-days at work.

Honestly, I didn't know we had a show choir until Principal Davis announced their victory. I guess it's kind of like a singing and dancing chorus group that sometimes wears costumes.

Even if I *wanted* to be in show choir, I'm not sure my parents would shell out the cash for it. It's like two hundred bucks a month because of all the travelling and food expenses. That's one thousand eight hundred dollars for the entire year!

Yeah, pretty sure my folks wouldn't be into that.

But it's cool. Getting a half-day at the mall was good enough for me.

It was almost noon on Friday. Students were to grab some food from the cafeteria, eat their lunch, and then gather outside to board the buses that were going to drive them to the mall.

I was in the lunch line trying to decide between a piece

of pizza or a taco. If I took the pizza, I'd feel full until dinner. If I took the taco, then I'd be happy, but still hungry… and also burp up tacos for the rest of the day.

Yuck, right? Pizza it was.

I set the plate of pizza on my tray and began walking, but stopped because of the small traffic jam. A girl at the front of the line was leaning against the dessert table, holding a cell phone high over her head. She pressed her lips together and made a weird kissy face before snapping a picture.

After the photo, she pushed her cell phone back into her purse, paid for her food, and disappeared into the cafeteria.

I got to the cashier and stared at the keypad so I could punch in my code for lunch. Our school was on an automated system that didn't require any cash for our food. Our parents sent the school a check and the balance was added to our account. All students had to do was punch in their code and that paid for their lunch.

The school still had to put someone behind the register to keep things running smoothly. That, and some students still paid with cash anyway. The boy in charge was wearing a tag that said his name was Jesse, and to ask him about their tomatoes.

It had only been a week since the whole "horseshoe" incident with the Soda Jerk and Cob.

There's no need for me to go too much into detail, but needless to say, Cob is no longer the head of Glitch.

COB
EX-LEADER
OF GLITCH

HE'S
SEEN
BETTER
DAYS...

Glitch, for those just joining our program, is the secret agency that recruited me awhile back. At first I thought it was kind of a joke or just some kind of club that a bunch of bored kids created, but it turns out the agency is legit, with more secrets than there are hairs on your head... unless you're bald, in which case... um, I'm sorry?

And Cob was Glitch's fearless leader, but after a couple of poorly made decisions, he got booted from the agency. Basically, he tried to give everyone at Buchanan head lice. I know, right? *Not cool.*

He was a couple places behind me in line at that moment, and he looked awful. At least as awful as a sixth grader could look. He used to look so professional, but after losing his position in Glitch, he sorta just let himself go.

Cob's clothes looked smudged and wrinkled, like he had picked them up off the floor of his garage after waking up. His hair was a hot mess, unkempt and greasy. And his glasses were fogged up and crooked on his face.

I couldn't help but feel sorry for him, even though he tried to give me head lice.

Farther behind Cob was Christopher Moss, AKA Christmas.

MOSS, CHRISTOPHER A.K.A. "CHRISTMAS"
LEADER OF THE SECRET AGENCY "SUCKERPUNCH"

Christmas was the leader of the rival secret agency in the school called Suckerpunch. This kid could be considered dangerous.

He was what was known as a "super sixth grader," which meant that he was held back a year for some reason, having to repeat the sixth grade. He used to be a member of Glitch, but was dropped when he started his second year of sixth grade.

Because of that, he created his own agency and proudly bragged about how Suckerpunch only existed to wreak havoc and cause chaos at Buchanan. It was his own way of getting back at the system.

The first time I met Christmas, he offered me a place in Suckerpunch. I'm proud to say that I politely declined.

When I saw him in line, I looked away before he noticed, hoping he wasn't looking at me. There was just something about the kid that got me all nervous inside. I don't know – maybe I was just afraid of him.

And then, sitting somewhere above Glitch and Suckerpunch was something that Cob called the "powers that be." Being new to Glitch, I had no idea what he was talking about, but surprisingly, neither did anyone else.

"Anytime now," Jesse said, bringing my head back down from the clouds.

I glanced over my shoulder at the other kids waiting impatiently with their lunch trays.

"Um," I said sheepishly. "Sorry." Then I tried to make conversation while punching my code into the number pad. "How 'bout those tomatoes?" I asked.

Jesse made a wonky face. "Why would you ask me a question like that? Do I look like some sort of tomato expert?" he replied, pronouncing the word "tomato" all weird, like "tah-mah-toe." Who does that?

I stumbled over my words. "Your button... the one on your apron... it says to ask about your tomatoes."

Jesse glanced down at the button. "Oh, yeah, that thing. I don't know anything about our tomatoes. They make us wear these pins when it's our turn to volunteer for this stuff."

"Oh," I said. I guess I wasn't sure why I expected an actual response about the tomatoes.

The number pad blipped at me, letting me know my food had been paid for. I picked up my tray, thanked the cashier, and headed out the door to the cafeteria.

Everyone was crazy loud when I stepped foot into the lunchroom, which wasn't surprising since we knew we were all going to the mall in less than twenty minutes. Giving kids a half-day at school was a sure-fire way of getting them all jacked with way too much energy.

I pumped an unhealthy amount of ketchup next to my

fries at the condiments table. The way I see it, there are two types of kids in this world – those who put ketchup *next* to their fries, and those who put ketchup *on top* of their fries.

After pumping out about a cup and a half of ketchup, I spun around and eyeballed the rest of the room, hoping to find a spot with my friends from Glitch.

Before I joined the secret agency, I always sat with Linus, the new leader of the agency. That was back when I didn't know anything about Glitch or Suckerpunch or Christmas – back when things were boring and normal. There was a big part of me that missed those days.

Back then, Linus and I would just sit in the cafeteria and argue about which comic book artist was better, or share secrets about leveling up faster in whatever video game we were absorbed in at the time.

We don't spend much time talking like that anymore.

After scanning the room like some sort of robot from outer space, I couldn't find any of my friends anywhere. And this was after I made a couple laps around the outside edge of the cafeteria. I'm sure other kids were starting to notice that I was just walking with my food instead of eating it. If I didn't take a seat soon, someone would say something to me for sure.

Too bad there weren't any completely empty tables. I had to resort to sitting at the end of a table that had some extra room. The other end was filled with all the cool girls in school. And not just the *kind of* cool girls, but the super duper popular ones. The ones who were cheerleaders and clothing models and somehow had amazing singing voices.

One of the girls sitting on the tabletop leaned back and stared at me. My presence somehow affected the air around her and she was annoyed.

She shot me a quick smirk, and then leaned forward again, rejoining the conversation her friends were having.

Maybe she wasn't annoyed after all.

I was so caught up with the cool girl that I didn't even notice the other girl who had taken a seat right across from me. It was like she materialized out of thin air, like some kind of creepy spirit ninja or something.

It was K-pop, and I was totes relieved to see her there.

K-pop was another member of Glitch who I had only met a week ago. She was trendy, cute, and had this kind of awesome energy to her that made her, like… electric or something.

Her headphones were hanging on her neck, but still playing her favorite Korean pop music loudly enough that anyone within three feet could hear it. That was why her nickname was K-pop – because she was obsessed with Korean pop music.

Whenever K-pop was around, I felt a little shy. I don't know if it's because I'm intimidated by her confidence or the way she smiled at me.

"Heyyyyyyy, girrrrrrl," I said. Yeah. My dumb brain made *that* come out of my mouth.

K-pop's eyes narrowed at me, like she was trying to understand a game I *wasn't* playing. "Heyyyy.... boyyyyyy?" she said slowly, raising the pitch of her voice at the end so it sounded like she was asking a question.

"Sorry," I said, stuffing a handful of fries into my mouth, hoping that a mouth full of fried potato sticks would distract me from saying anything else stupid. "What's the haps?" I asked.

"Bad things," K-pop said, leaning closer.

I looked over my shoulder at the rest of the sixth graders making loud noises behind me. "What kind of bad things?"

When she didn't answer, I looked back… and she was gone.

But not creepy-gone this time. She had just gotten up and was walking to the doors at the side of the cafeteria.

On the table in front of me was a small slip of paper folded in half.

Sliding my hand across the cold table, I held my thumb down on the corner of the paper, and pushed the other side open with my first finger.

All it said was, "Backstage. Now."

I folded the note up and brought it closer to me. Half of me was worried about what K-pop wanted me backstage for, but the other half of me was excited and hopeful.

You see, since Cob left Glitch, the agency basically fell apart. Glitch has helped me learn a lot about myself, and it was beginning to feel like home. The other agents actually felt like part of my family.

Linus is a nice guy, but it was Maddie that really helped me become a better agent. And to be honest, she's cool enough in school that she doesn't need new friends. It's because of Glitch that Maddie even spoke to me in the first place.

And now that the agency was barely holding on by a string, I was beginning to worry that the friends I made there would go off and do their own thing, leaving me all alone.

The note K-pop had delivered told me to go backstage. The only stage that Buchanan School had was at the front of the cafeteria, so it wasn't like my walk took that long.

After tossing my food in the garbage, I snuck off to the side of the lunchroom to where the entrance of the stage was. The huge velvet curtain was shut so nobody could see what was happening behind it.

When I rounded the corner and got to the side of the

stage, I could see four other kids standing around a small foldout table arguing about something. The only light was from a small lamp on the table pointing down and bathing everything in a soft yellow glow.

K-POP SAID I COULDN'T POST AN IMAGE OF GLITCH, SO SHE GAVE ME THIS STOCK PHOTO OF BUSINESS PEOPLE CROSSING THEIR ARMS AND SMILING INSTEAD. I GUESS ADULTS SPEND A LOT OF TIME DOING THESE THINGS? TRY IT. IT'S WEIRD.

K-pop was already there with her arms crossed.

A boy named Janky was standing next to her, nodding his head and jabbing his thumb in the air in her direction.

Janky and K-pop were best friends, and he was the newest member of Glitch, even though he said he didn't want to be a part of it originally. Guess he changed his mind, but you won't hear me complain – it means I'm no longer the noob on the team!

Linus, the new leader of Glitch, was moving his hands around like he was trying to make a point. I couldn't hear what he was saying, but I could tell he wasn't happy about it.

And then Maddie was the last behind the table. She was standing with her hands on her hips staring out into space, listening to everything that Linus said, like she was soaking it in. She also looked pretty upset.

Maddie was one of my newest best friends. She was there on the first day I had been involved in anything that had to do with Glitch, and she had stuck beside me in every case I fumbled with. She was really the only reason I had gotten through any of it.

She was the kind of girl who really knew what she was doing, even when she didn't. Maddie doesn't wait around and hope for things to blow over – she takes action and fixes those things instead of doing nothing.

Plus she was super cute and I *might* or *might not* have a crush on her.

Maddie was the first to notice me at the side of the dark stage. My heart warmed when we made eye contact, and I tossed out a smile.

"Good of you to *finally* join us," Maddie said, annoyed and *not* smiling.

I guess her heart wasn't in the same place as mine.

"I only got a note, like, a minute ago," I said, setting K-pop's slip of paper on the table that everyone stood around.

The only other thing on the table was Linus's cell phone.

"I texted you," Maddie huffed.

"No, you didn't," I said, pulling my phone from my front pocket. "My phone never—" I stopped talking when I saw that I had fifteen unread texts between Maddie and Linus. "Whoops."

"That's fine," Linus said strongly, straightening his

back. "At least you're here now. We have a bit of a situation."

"K-pop told me," I said, and then added, "Well, she didn't tell me the situation. She just told me that there *was* a situation. Or something bad or whatever. What's going on?"

Maddie walked a few feet away, toward the back of the stage, to a large white foam board that had some black writing all over it. The stage was too dark for me to read what was on the sign, but the stink of magic marker floated under my nose.

"We've got an assignment for you," Maddie said from the darker corner of the stage as she lifted the foam board.

"I received orders right before lunch," Linus said.

Before he could explain, I interrupted. "*You* received orders? Aren't you the one who *gives* orders now? What're you talking about?"

Linus paused, taking a deep breath.

K-pop and Janky remained silent as Maddie shuffled the foam board around.

"I got a text from a blocked number right before lunch," Linus said. "It had instructions on what we're supposed to do."

"An unknown number?" I asked. "Was it Cob?"

"No," Linus replied. "Cob was nearby when I got the message, and he wasn't messing with his phone. This is someone else."

"Okay," I said. "What did the message say?"

Another pause and a deep breath, and Linus continued. He pointed at the foam board that Maddie was holding. She was now next to the table. "The message said that someone from Glitch had to walk around the cafeteria wearing this sign."

I read the sign, feeling my heart drop at the message that was written on it.

"But…" I said, "This could start some trouble. Like, some *serious* trouble."

The other four kids sat there, silently agreeing with me.

"Okay, so we just won't do it," I said. "Why is this even something we're discussing?" I looked at Maddie. "Why'd you even *make* the sign to begin with? You're not seriously considering doing this, are you?"

Linus spoke up. "Look, Brody, I'm the new leader of Glitch, and I'm deciding that this is something we have to do. Someone out there knows this agency is struggling to stick around, and they're messing with us. Well, I want to deliver the message that we're *not* an agency to be messed with. Glitch is still just as strong as ever."

"But—" was the only word I said before Linus cut me off.

"We're doing this!" he said, pointing a finger at my face. "One of us is going to wear this sign while the rest of us keep an eye out for whoever it was that sent the text! I bet that whoever sent it will be somewhere in the cafeteria watching his dumb little prank make everyone angry. So all we gotta do is look for some kid who's snickering off to the side of the lunchroom."

I shook my head, not sure of what else to say. I thought it was crazy for us to go along with the prank, but Linus thought the opposite. I wasn't in the mood to argue. I mean, he was the leader of Glitch, which meant he had the most experience out of all the kids on stage at that moment. That's gotta count for something, right?

"Whoever's wearing this sign might as well kiss their pretty face goodbye," I said sarcastically. And then I asked, "So who's gonna wear it?"

Again, the four other members of the agency stood silently, but this time they weren't staring at nothing. They were staring at me.

"Of course," I said. I would've totally refused if it

weren't for the fact that I really didn't want to watch Glitch fall apart. "Welp, better help me get it on then."

About two minutes later, I was at the center of the stage, just behind the slit in the curtain. I hadn't walked out into the lunchroom just yet because I wasn't exactly ready to face the last few minutes of my life.

The foam board was heavier than I would've guessed it to be, and actually, there were *two* foam boards. One to hang down the front of me, and one to hang down my back. Maddie made two straps out of duct tape to hang the boards over my shoulders.

"Go already!" Linus ordered impatiently.

"Gimme a minute!" I said.

"What're you waiting for?" he asked.

"I'm waiting for one of you to tell me this is crazy and that I *shouldn't* do it!" I answered.

K-pop laughed. "Quit being a baby and get out there! Janky and Maddie are waiting near the exits. Once you step outside, it'll be obvious who sent the text because they'll probably be the first ones laughing and pointing!"

"*Probably*," I repeated, pushing one side of the curtain open.

I could already see the bustling cafeteria of kids. Everyone was having a grand ol' time, laughing and joking with one another, waiting for the announcement to fill the buses outside.

Sucking air through my nose, I peeled the curtain back. "Here goes nothing," I whispered.

I hopped off the stage with eyes wide open. I looked like one of those tiny monkeys you see in animal books – the ones whose eyes were bigger than their brains.

At first, nobody noticed me. A couple kids glanced in

my direction and giggled, but nothing that made me worried just yet. I mean, the message on the sign was pretty clear so it wasn't like people were going to ignore me. Whoever sent the text knew that much, and it was obvious that they wanted to cause some sort of trouble.

Hand written in magic marker on the front and back of the boards I was wearing was this: *The Buchanan football team is lame.*

It wasn't as if our football team was anything to call home about, but I knew the kids on the team would very much disagree with that statement while using their fists to argue their point.

So yeah, since all the sixth graders were waiting in the lunchroom until it was time to leave, you can bet that the *entire* football team was there.

At least they were on the other side of the cafeteria so hopefully Linus could pull me away before any knuckle punch sandwiches were served.

Maddie was across the room, darting her head back and forth, trying to see if any of the students looked suspicious as I made my way down one of the aisles.

Janky was on the other side of the cafeteria… *munching on a blueberry muffin?* He wasn't even *trying* to help out!

Back at the slit in the curtain, K-pop and Linus were scanning the crowd.

None of them looked like they had *any* kind of leads on who sent the mystery text!

Suddenly someone stepped right in front of me, blocking my path. I must've been more scared than I realized because I totally flinched.

"Um, what're you doing?" the boy asked.

It was another student in the school named Chase Cooper. He's someone I would consider a friend of mine, but not a super close friend. I mean, he's got his group that he hangs out with, and I've got my own group, but he's still one of those guys I wouldn't mind talking comics with. How I wished *this* were one of those times.

"Dude," Chase said, looking around, making sure I hadn't gotten too much attention yet. "*What*… are you doing?"

"Oh, y'know, just hanging out," I said, trying to make a joke. "I'd really like to start a new fashion trend."

Chase chuckled, which made me feel a little better. "I don't think black eyes would make a very good trend. Can you imagine getting ready for school with a couple punches to the face?"

"If it took off, I bet someone would make a machine that would do it for you!" I said. "Wake up, brush your teeth, fix your hair, get punched in the eye... or *eyes*."

"No way," Chase argued. "I'd rather have my alarm clock do the punching! That's one way to wake up plus I wouldn't have to sit through breakfast knowing I'd have to get punched eventually."

I sighed, remembering why we were even joking about getting beaten up. "That's a *horrible* way to start the day."

"Right?" Chase said. "Which is making me wonder why you're looking for something like that during lunch?"

I peeked over at the football team. They still had no idea I was walking around with the foam board.

"Look," I said to Chase. "I know it sounds crazy, but I *have* to wear this sign right now."

"You *have* to?" Chase asked. "Why?"

I paused, wondering the exact same question. "Y'know, I actually have no idea."

Linus was still searching over the crowd for whoever sent the mystery text message. I'd already been walking around for a good minute or two. If he hadn't found anyone yet, I doubt that he was ever going to.

Looking at Maddie, I saw that she also had nothing. She shrugged her shoulders at me. Not a good sign.

Janky was still chewing on a mouthful of muffins.

"*Are you serious?*" came a shout from a few tables over.

I spun around, hoping the shout wasn't about me.

But I was so wrong that it hurt.

At once, half the football team walked across the lunch tables, like, on *top* of the tables, until they popped onto the floor in front of me. They weren't bigger than me or anything, but when they're all in a group, I don't see individual kids. I see one giant machine, like they had all somehow hooked together to create a single monster.

I expected Chase to disappear, but he didn't. He stayed right next to me the whole time.

The boy leading the football players walked right up to me. I knew him. Most of the school did. He was the star football player on the team – the "quarterfront," I think it's called? Quarterback? Maybe that was it.

His name was Jake, and the kids behind him – the other members of the football team – were part of his little group that called themselves the wolf pack.

With both of his hands, he pushed against the foam board on my chest, making me stumble back a little.

"You think we're lame, huh?" Jake sneered.

"No, man!" I said. "I don't even know if you guys are any good or not!"

He jabbed at the foam board with his finger, making a "THOK" sound. "That's not what your pretty little sign says."

24

THIS IS JAKE. HE'S THE STAR QB FOR BUCHANAN. HE DOESN'T ACTUALLY HAVE SKULLS FOR EYES ...OR MAYBE HE DOES... OKAY, HE DOESN'T. ...OR DOES HE??? NO . YES . MAYBE?

My brain was starting to freeze up. I had no idea what to say. Who in their right mind would walk around a cafeteria wearing a ridiculous sign like this? …don't answer that.

"It's just, um…" I said, stuttering because I was suddenly aware that *everyone* in the cafeteria was waiting for me to explain myself. Where were all the teachers? How come no one was trying to step in? Oh, right. They were all outside the lunchroom, getting ready for a tidal wave of students to pour into the buses.

"Well?" Jake shouted, pushing against the sign on my body again.

A girl near the front doors of the cafeteria bounced to her feet, cupped her hands over her mouth, and shouted, "*Oh, snap! Foooooood fiiiiight!*" And then she pitched a golf ball sized roll across the room, nailing the center of the sign I was wearing. It fell to the floor with a pitiful sound.

For a couple seconds, everyone was staring at the girl who threw the bread. She stood only for a moment before returning to her seat, embarrassed.

Jake shook his head at the girl, as if somehow she was immature for throwing a roll across the room. I know, right? Like someone looking for an *actual* fight is better than someone looking for a *food* fight.

Chase stepped between Jake and me. "Leave him alone," he said.

Jake stared daggers into Chase's eyes. It was one of the most intense standoffs I'd ever seen, like hardcore, almost as if there was more going on between them than just some random kid wearing a sign.

Jake blinked. He flicked his fingers in front of his face. "You're like a gnat that won't go away," he said. "Every time I turn around, you're there, flying in front of my face, annoying the spew outta me."

"Maybe if you weren't such a rotten apple, I'd just fly away and leave you alone," Chase said.

I'm not gonna lie, that burn gave me goose bumps.

Jake grinned snidely as he sidestepped Chase. Pointing at me, Jake continued, "So you think you can do better than us?"

"Better at football?" I asked, looking back at the curtain to see if Linus was going to do anything, but he wasn't even there anymore. "No, man. It's nothing like that!" I said to Jake.

"Then what?" Jake said, jabbing at the foam board again. "Why would you walk around here with such hurtful words written on a sign?"

Jake was right. Even though he was the one looking for trouble, it was only because *I* was the one offering it.

26

"I'll take it off," I said, gripping the straps on my shoulders.

"Oh, no you don't," Jake said, snapping his fingers at his wolf pack behind him. "Allow *us* to take it off."

At Jake's snapping finger, his friends snarled like they were wolves. Was it strange to see a bunch of sixth graders act like that? Yes. Did it make everything *that much* scarier for me? Yes, again.

Jake crossed his arms and stood like a statue as the other members of the football team darted past him. I stumbled, and I'm pretty sure I let out a super high-pitched squeal.

At that moment, Chase grabbed one of the straps on my shoulder and yanked me around in a full circle as some of the wolf pack dove to the ground, barely missing me.

"Run!" Chase said, still gripping my shoulder strap so I wouldn't lose my balance.

I didn't waste any time, jumping up onto the lunch table as kids shouted all around me. Chase was right behind me on the floor.

"Get out into the lobby!" he shouted. "I'll try to keep them from following you!"

Leaping off the table, I landed on my feet like I was some kind of action hero, and trust me when I say that *I* was just as surprised as everyone else that I didn't biff.

Sprinting toward the front of the cafeteria, I tore the boards off my body and let them fall to the ground. Some of the wolf pack that had gotten past Chase slipped on the signs, sliding along the floor like they were on hoverboards. For a second, I felt a little jealous because it kind of looked like fun.

Finally, I saw Linus and Maddie holding the door open at the front of the cafeteria, motioning for me to slow down, which I *would've* done, except that I was running at near light speed.

Linus was shouting for me to stop, but he knew I wasn't going to. I could tell from the way his voice cracked.

Maddie screamed. Or maybe it was me. There was so much noise that it was hard to tell! Let's just say… at one point during my speedy escape… *someone* screamed like a baby…

…whatever, it was me, okay?

The instant my foot hit the carpet in the lobby, I tripped, rolling across the floor like a rag doll that a two year old hated. Everyone out there backed away so I wouldn't knock 'em down like they were bowling pins.

Finally, when I came to a stop, I was on my back staring at the clouds through the skylight in the ceiling. It would've been pretty relaxing if it weren't for all the rug burns on my knees and elbows.

The other sixth graders around me had a short laugh, but went about their business pretty quickly after I had skidded to a stop.

Maddie, Linus, and K-pop were hovering above me, and for a second, I wondered if I was looking up from the inside of a coffin at my funeral.

"Nice one," Maddie joked, holding up a cell phone and wallet that looked exactly like mine.

K-pop lifted her hands over me, showing me a pair of tennis shoes that also struck a resemblance to the ones I owned.

And then Linus waved a couple of pens over my face. "I think these are all yours."

The moment he said that, I felt a draft on my shoeless feet. I had crashed so hard that all my stuff flew off me and out of my pockets.

"Dude," K-pop laughed. "That biff was a full-on yard sale!"

"A what?" I asked.

"A yard sale," K-pop repeated. "It's when your crash is so incredibly epic that all your stuff flies away from you and spreads out behind you, kind of like you're having a yard sale."

"Oh," I said, not too excited about the term.

"Son, are you alright?" came Principal Davis's voice from behind my friends.

"Yeah," I said, embarrassed and sitting up. "I just, um... fell."

Jake and his wolf pack were standing right inside the doors of the cafeteria, just staring at me. If Principal Davis wasn't around, I'm sure they would've been on me like cheese on macaroni. Like ketchup on fries. Like the skin on chicken... or any other animal. You get the point.

"Then get your shoes on and get in line," the principal said, waving his hand toward the front doors of the school. He seemed more upset than concerned, probably because he was trying to herd an entire class of 6th graders into several long, yellow buses. "We're starting to load up."

K-pop dropped my tennis shoes next to my feet. "Nice socks," she said.

I looked down, remembering that I had worn my favorite pair of superhero socks that day. "What?" I said, slipping my tennis shoes back over my feet. I was embarrassed enough to let my mouth starting running. "Sometimes I wear socks with comic book pictures all over them. It wasn't a gym day for me so I wasn't going to take my shoes off at all today! How was I to know they were gonna try escaping the clutches of my eleven-year-old feet? I bet you'd laugh if I told you I had matching underwear too, huh? Huh?"

Maddie tightened her lips and furrowed her brow. "Too. Much. Information. Dude."

Linus and K-pop were holding tears back.

Chase was still in the cafeteria, hunched over by the door, and waving a thumbs-up at me. I lifted my arm, and found enough strength to muster a thumbs-up back at him.

Janky somehow appeared out of nowhere, still chewing on a mouthful of muffin. "S'up, guys?" he asked, and then he gave me a thumbs-up as well. "Nice yard sale, by the way."

"Great," I said, standing to my feet and nursing my raw elbows. "Am I the only one who's never heard that term before?"

Just outside the school, all the sixth graders had gathered on the front sidewalks, looking for the bus they had been assigned to.

"So was all that worth anything?" I asked, shuffling my

feet along the concrete.

Linus shook his head, sighing. "I didn't see anyone who looked suspicious. Did any of you guys?"

Maddie, K-pop, and Janky all shook their heads at the same time. K-pop was furiously texting away on her cell phone.

"Then it was for nothing," I stated.

"Maybe," Linus said. "I guess that would be the best case scenario."

"Best case scenario?" I repeated.

"Sure," K-pop agreed without looking up from her phone. "If it was just a prank, then it's over with."

"Ugh," I grunted, wanting to argue because I had just been through heck and didn't want it to be for nothing. "What about Christmas? Suckerpunch? Could they have sent the text to mess with us?"

Linus shrugged his shoulder. "Maybe," he said simply. "The number was unknown so we don't know for sure."

"K-pop has her ways around that," Maddie said.

"You mean, like, hacking?" Janky asked. "Or, like, *double*-hacking?"

"Double-hacking isn't a thing," K-pop said.

"Oh," Janky said, hanging his head a bit. "I don't know much about computers, I guess."

K-pop's voice softened as she raised her eyebrows at Janky, but her eyes never left the screen of her cell phone. "This has nothing to do with hacking. It's all phone games."

"Who are you texting all the time?" I asked, curious.

"My bestie," K-pop said.

Janky slightly moved his head as if he was shocked at K-pop's response.

She lowered her phone and looked at him. "My *girl* bestie. You're my *boy* bestie, Janky! And you always will be.

I'm just texting Gidget."

Janky didn't say anything. He just smiled and let out a sigh of relief.

"Gidget?" I asked. "That's her name?"

K-pop nodded quickly, returning her attention to her cell phone.

"Valentine?" a man's voice said.

I looked up from where I was standing. It was Mr. Lien. The *grumpy* Mr. Lien. Not the *cheerful* Mr. Lien.

Buchanan School has two Mr. Liens. One is named Allen Lien, while the other is named Nick Lien. The way people told them apart when talking about them was to include their first initial in their name.

So it was Mr. A. Lien who was talking to me from the bus. Everyone always joked that it sounded like we called him Mr. Alien, but those jokes were only fueled by the fact that he was also the weirdest dude in the world.

He never made eye contact with anyone – students or other teachers. And he was always speaking softly to himself. Some kids believed he was sent here from another planet to observe humans and that he was speaking through a secret communicator when he talked under his breath.

He's never been seen eating lunch, or at least, like, actual *human* food. He carries around a metal canteen that drips dark green liquid when he slurps from the spout. Is it probably juiced up vegetables? Maybe. But who's to say it's not ground up alien food for his super creepy alien organs?

I don't think there's any way to prove one way or the other.

"Valentine," Mr. A. Lien said again. "You're on my bus. Get on, sit down, and keep your mouth shut."

See? He was the grumpy one.

"Find us at the mall," Maddie said as she boarded her

bus. "We'll all meet in the food court."

I gave her a smile for good luck, because that's what secret agents do, right? Right? Anyone?

"On the bus!" Mr. A. Lien commanded again.

Without wanting to get yelled at for a third time, I climbed up the steps and looked for a good place to sit. Normally I'd sit near the back, but it was already packed.

Have I ever mentioned how unlucky of a kid I am? If not, just let it go on record right now that I think the universe hates me and is constantly out to get me.

As if Mr. A. Lien on my bus wasn't bad enough, Jake and his entire wolf pack were also on there taking up all the seats in the rear.

Best. Day. Ever.

I fell right into one of the empty seats in front before Jake or his wolf pack saw me. Sliding my butt way down, I hunched over, curled up in a little ball, and stared out the window. Jake and his crew were at least twenty seats behind me, so as long as I stayed quiet and out of sight, it was going to be a decent trip.

Mr. A. Lien stomped his way up the steps. He held a clipboard in front of him, tapping it and speaking under his breath, *probably* counting the students, but *possibly* talking to his alien BFFs.

Finally, the bus pulled away from the school. Shouts of joy came from all the students behind me. I would've joined them, but was too scared that Jake might see me. Instead, I just sunk even lower into my seat.

Mr. A. Lien took the seat in front of me, staring straight ahead and moving his lips, talking to himself again. It was pretty common for him to do that sort of thing, and when it happened, most of the kids in class knew they could get away with anything because he just wasn't paying attention.

The students behind me grew louder and louder, joking with each other as the bus lurched around the corner and onto the street. We were officially on our way to the mall and away from Buchanan School.

"No more school! No more school!" Jake chanted.

Being the popular jock he was, everyone on the bus joined in.

My phone buzzed in my pocket. When I pulled it out, I saw that I had a text from Maddie.

"*Saw Jake on your bus,*" she had typed. "*We'll be @ the mall soon enough. Don't die.*"

My phone buzzed again, this time with a picture message. When I clicked the message, a selfie of Maddie and K-pop appeared. They both had goofy grins on their faces. It was enough to make me laugh.

"*LOL. I'll do my best to stay alive,*" I typed back, smashing the "send" button with my thumb.

Just then, Jake's voice cut through all the noise and chaos of the other students. "Look at *this* loser!"

A wave of fear washed over me as I shut my eyes. I knew I'd mess up. Somehow he had seen me at the front of the bus, and was about to unleash his wolf pack on me.

I was so far down in my seat though! How was it possible that he saw me at all?

And then Jake shouted again. "Look at this kid and his playing cards!"

Obviously, I didn't have any cards in my hands so he was talking about someone else on the bus.

Slowly and carefully, I lifted my head so my eyes were above the top of my seat. Jake and his wolf pack were still at the back of the bus, but Jake was hovering over a random kid back there.

I recognized the boy from a few of my classes, but can honestly say I'd never said a word to him. He was always the first one in the room and always in the chair closest to the exit, which was also always the seat at the very back of the class.

His name was Edgar. Most kids would want to use "Ed" as a nickname, but not this dude. He insisted on his full name.

He was quiet 99% of the time, and when he walked the halls between classes, he kept his hands straight down on both sides, moved quickly, and always stared at the ground.

He was bigger than a lot of the other kids at Buchanan. Taller and thicker than everyone else. Being the size that he was, I was surprised he wasn't on the football team until I remembered that football wasn't for everyone. We all have our own hobbies, and Edgar's hobby *wasn't* being on the team. Apparently *his* hobby had something to do with playing cards, which was awesome.

Edgar definitely wasn't one of the "cool" kids in school, but that didn't mean anything because he wasn't trying to be a "cool" kid. He was just trying to make it through middle school like everyone else. Like me.

And on that bus, he was getting picked on for being different.

I bit my lip, listening to Jake and his wolf pack spout off insult after insult in Edgar's direction. At first, the bus full of students nervously laughed about it, with a slight chuckle here and there, but it soon grew into much more than that.

I peeked over the top of my bench again. Edgar wasn't even doing anything. He was just sitting in his seat, staring out the window at the passing scenery as Jake ran his mouth.

It looked like Edgar was ignoring Jake, but I could tell that he was just getting more embarrassed.

I fell into my seat again, looking at the back of Mr. A.

Lien's head, hoping the teacher would say something, but he was completely zoned out.

If I just sat silently, the bus would get to the mall, and I'd be able to jump off, safe from Jake and his wolf pack.

But that would mean they'd keep picking on Edgar…

If I stood up and said anything at all, then Jake would totally shift his attention to me!

Gah! Decisions, decisions!

But truthfully, it only took me half a second to decide what to do because I had already made the decision long ago. When I first joined Glitch, I made the decision to do the right thing in any situation, no matter what.

The scene from the cafeteria flashed in my mind again, and I realized that Chase stood next to me when it was easier for him to stay out of it.

And right then, Edgar needed me to stand by him.

I opened my mouth to shout, but froze for a second, not sure of what to even say. Finally, and without using any common sense at all, I shouted at the top of my lungs, "Vampires exist! I've seen them with my own two eyes!"

Everyone stared. I was met with confused faces of other sixth graders, except for one kid near the middle of his bus sitting alone in a seat. His name was Brayden, and I think he was kind of an expert on monsters.

"Darn right!" Brayden shouted.

Jake was at the back of the bus, shaking his head at me. At least his attention was off of Edgar.

The wolf pack leaned over, glaring at me. Jake narrowed his eyes like he needed glasses, but wasn't wearing them.

Even Edgar had stopped staring out the window to look at me.

And I just kind of stood there, not sure of what to do or say next. All I wanted was for Jake to leave Edgar alone, but I hadn't thought far enough ahead to do anything else.

"Um," I said. "S'up, guys?"

Jake's eyes went from me, to the back of Mr. A. Lien's head, and then to me again. He stepped sideways into the narrow aisle of the bus and started clumsily walking toward the front.

I stayed in my seat, watching as the leader of the wolf pack made his way toward me. What was he thinking? He wasn't seriously going to start trouble right in front of the alien teacher, was he?

Then again, would the alien posing as a human even care? Mr. A. Lien's got bigger fish to fry – like planning the invasion of our home planet.

The bus was dead silent. The only sound was coming from the rush of traffic in the streets and the engine switching gears. It was the most awkward silence a school bus had ever heard.

My neck muscles twitched as I could only watch Jake come closer. He wasn't saying anything, and he wasn't blinking also.

The bus turned the corner sharply. I could hear the gears grinding against each other as my body tensed up in the right places to keep me from falling over.

Jake was only a few seats away from me, and I had nowhere to go. Mr. A. Lien was still muttering nonsense to himself as the rest of the students kept their eyes peeled for what was bound to be the talk of the school for weeks.

Only one seat away from me, Jake took another step.

And then, all of a sudden, the school bus lurched forward, nearly screeching to a complete stop.

Jake fell forward on his face in the middle of the aisle. I was only still standing because my back smashed into the seat that Mr. A. Lien was sitting in.

The mall entrance was right outside the window along with a bunch of other students that were waiting for the rest of Buchanan School to arrive.

The driver flung open the door of the bus, turned around in his seat, and pointed at a sign near the mirror above his head. "Get off my bus! Ain't nobody gonna throw fists on my boat! I've gone all year without an incident *or* a fight and I'm gonna go the rest of the year without one!"

The sign he was pointing at said, "92 days without trouble." The number 92 was handwritten with a dry erase marker.

Jake wiped his chin and pushed himself off the floor. Mr. Lien turned his head like a confused deer, watching as the leader of the wolf pack dusted himself off.

"This isn't over," Jake whispered to me before stepping off the bus.

I let out a *humongous* sigh of relief. That could've been bad. Like *real* bad.

Catching my breath, I waited for the rest of the bus to unload before getting up. I just sat staring out the window, happy that Jake and his wolf pack decided to go into the mall rather than wait for me.

"Hey, man," Edgar's voice said from above. He was the last person in line.

"Hey," I said.

Edgar tightened a smile. He wasn't looking me in the eye. "Thanks... for that."

I knew he was embarrassed, and I didn't want to make it worse for him. "For what? I just wanted to let everyone know that vampires exist. Just knowing that might save their lives someday."

Edgar laughed. "Right," he said as he hopped off the bus.

I followed behind him, but didn't say anything else. I figured it was better to just let the whole thing go instead of trying to say *thanks* and *you're welcome* and *blah, blah, blah.*

As everyone pushed themselves through the doors of the mall, teachers were lined up both outside and inside, taking attendance and making sure everyone was there.

Above the entrance of the mall was a sign that had a picture of a gorilla's face on it. The gorilla was the logo for the mall we were at, which I guess meant that people were supposed to shop like animals? I don't know. It was weird, and I didn't care about understanding it.

The mall was called the "Gorilla Villa." Kinda dorky, right? That's what they get for trusting the name of a shopping center to an underpaid twenty-two year old designer. At least, I think that's what they get. I'm not sure about the whole designer thing though – it's just something I've heard my dad complain about before.

As soon as Principal Davis checked my name off the list, I walked farther into the mall where most of the other students had already clumped together with their friends.

Pushing my hands deep into my pockets, I lowered my head and starting walking to the food court where Maddie had told me to meet her.

Since it was a Friday afternoon, the mall was actually pretty busy. Shoppers walked in and out of stores carrying bags full of clothes and other random things they bought from one of the many stores.

The smell of garlic lingered from the Italian restaurant that was, strangely enough, *not* in the food court. I never understood why a food place would set up somewhere *other* than the food court. It pretty much guaranteed that spot in the mall was going to be available for rent within a few months.

As I continued my trek, a small train drove by me accompanied by a couple kids on bicycles that were designed to look like horses. It was odd, but super cool to see it.

The small train was a ride for younger kids to enjoy. It wasn't on actual tracks, but instead, had tires that were about the size of go-cart wheels. The dude driving it was decked out in a train conductor's uniform and kept ringing a bell on the engine.

The kids riding the bicycles were supposed to look like they were following the train on horses. The whole thing was moving slow enough to barely keep up with how fast I was walking.

Once I got to the center of the mall, the train turned the corner and continued down to the end of the building with the big fountain.

Our mall was pretty famous for the fountain. It was a giant marble circle with several streams of water shooting into the air. Small golden tiles lined the inside wall of the fountain, and lights under the water made the whole thing shimmer with gold and silver colors.

It was a little different than most normal fountains though because it was called the Silver Dollar Fountain. Anyone could throw money into the water if they wanted to, but most people threw silver dollars into it. Like, 90% of the coins at the bottom were silver dollars, which was another reason why the fountain glowed so brightly.

I know, right? Who walks around with silver dollars in the pocket? Well, on both sides of the fountain were machines that exchanged dollar bills for silver dollars. It became such a sign of good fortune to toss in a silver dollar that the fountain was a huge success.

The closer I got to the food court, the more my stomach rumbled. Because of all the garbage that happened in the school cafeteria, I barely got to eat any food, and the smell of pretzels and cheeseburgers were singing sweet songs to my nose holes.

The stage where the show choir was going to perform was right at the front of the food court, facing all the chairs and tables where people ate.

Right behind the stage was a giant black cauldron that looked like something a witch would use to brew weird and evil stews with eyeballs and rat-tails and other gross things.

GAZPACHO!
SAMPLES!
← SAMPLE LADY...
with her hand IN the soup!
VAT OF COLD SOUP

"Sample?" asked the woman next to the vat, which totally added to the "witch" vibe. She held out a white cup filled with red liquid. "Our Italian restaurant is at the other end of the mall, but we're here today giving out samples of our gazpacho. If you like it, there's plenty more where it came from," she explained with a smile.

Of course it was the restaurant that wasn't in the food court. It was pretty smart of them to hand out samples in the spot where everyone was already getting their food anyway. The woman was so kind that I felt bad for thinking her restaurant was doomed before it had a chance.

"Gazpacho?" I asked, taking the small white cup into my hand, and bringing it up to my mouth to take a sip.

She waited for me to taste the soup before explaining what it was. "*It's ice-cold vegetable soup!*"

The second the cold liquid hit my tongue, I pressed my lips together and sprayed it out of my mouth, all over the poor lady. It wasn't that the soup was gross. It was just that I was expecting some kind of warm tomato soup and when the freezing cold broth touched my tongue, I freaked!

The woman stood there, dripping with small drops of cold vegetable soup.

At this point, I'd love to tell you that I was mature about how I handled the incident, but I can't do that. I was so embarrassed that I set my cup back on her tray and walked away as fast as I could, but not before muttering, "*I'm sorry!*"

I didn't look back at the woman with the gazpacho samples, but I could feel her eyes burning holes in the back of my head like they were laser beams.

My friends were sitting only a few tables away, which I was thankful for because that meant I didn't have to walk aimlessly around the food court after that gazpacho accident.

Joining my friends, I sat in one of the chairs at their table and hunched over, nervously playing with a crusty spot on the table. Maddie, Linus, K-pop, and Janky were all there already.

"OMG, dude," K-pop said. "You could've kindly said '*no thank you*' for the sample back there."

"I didn't mean to do it!" I said defensively. "What's she doing?"

"I think she's casting a spell on you," K-pop said. "Right now, her lips are moving, and she's staring over here pointing a finger at you." She paused, gasping. "Her nails are long and nasty!"

"Seriously?"

"Oh, dude," Maddie coughed, putting her hand over her eyes. "She's coming over."

"No, she's not," I said, scared to death.

"She's saying something under her breath," K-pop continued with a shaky voice. "And dragging her finger across her throat!"

A chill shot through my entire body. "No, she's not!" I said, spinning in my chair. "I'm sorry, alright? I'm so so so—"

My friends were messing with me. The woman with the samples of gazpacho was smiling and handing out paper cups to the people who walked by her.

"I hate you guys," I said.

Linus chuckled. "Well, you're about to hate us even more."

"Why?" I asked.

He answered by sliding his cell phone across the table toward me. "I got another text from that unknown number."

"Nope," I said immediately. "I'm not wearing another stupid sign around the mall. The school is one thing, and I shouldn't even have done it there, but the mall? No way, man. I'm out."

Maddie pressed her lips to the side. "There's no sign this time," she said.

"No? Then what?" I asked.

"Read it," Linus said.

I picked up his cell phone and looked at the message. It was a picture of the baby carousel outside one of the nearby mall shops, along with a text message after it.

"Brody and Maddie have to take a selfie at the carousel, and then post it online… or else."

"Or else what?" I asked, sliding the phone back to Linus.

He shrugged his shoulders. "I don't know, but I'd rather not find out."

I looked Linus in the eye. "You actually want us to do this?" I asked him.

He nodded.

"No way, dude!" I said. "Whatever game this is isn't one I want to play! Whoever's sending those texts to you is messing with us! And I'm willing to bet everything that it's

46

Christmas!"

That time, Linus shook his head, pointing at a spot behind me. "Christmas has been sitting there the whole time. I've had my eye on him, and he hasn't touched his cell phone once."

"Dun, dun, dunnnnnn," K-pop sang dramatically.

I leaned back to look at Christmas, who was sitting at a table by himself, etching drawings with his thumbnail into the side of a Styrofoam cup. The tables around him were full of his Suckerpunch agents, all wearing black suits and sunglasses. Like, how was that not a red flag for teachers?

I mean, really? How the heck didn't the teachers at Buchanan School see this kid walking around surrounded by kids in suits? You'd think it'd be super obvious to them, but no! It was like the teachers didn't have a clue!

Just like back in the school kitchen, I looked away before Christmas noticed I was staring.

"Okay," I said. "If it's *not* Christmas, then it's obviously someone with a bag full of crazy that they're trying to dump on us."

Linus snatched his phone off the table and sat forward. "You don't have a choice," he said. "If you don't do this, then you're *out* of Glitch."

"*What?*" I said, confused. "Are you serious?"

"As serious as head lice," he replied.

Maddie, K-pop, and Janky sat silently, just as shocked as I was.

"You'd kick me out because of this?" I asked, just to be clear.

"In a heartbeat," Linus said coldly. "I'm the *leader* of Glitch right now, and I've got to make sure our members are just as committed as *I* am."

Maddie spoke up, but not to defend me. "Brody,

c'mon…"

"Who says I'm not committed?" I asked, annoyed with Linus.

"*You'd* say it by refusing this *mission*," Linus said, scowling.

"You mean this game?"

"We don't know that it's a game," Linus said, sitting back in his chair. "I *hope* it's just a game, but—"

Linus's phone buzzed, interrupting him.

"What's it say?" Maddie asked.

Linus swallowed hard, and then read the text. "Three minutes. The tock's clicking. I mean, the *clock's ticking*."

"All they want you to do is post a selfie," K-pop said with a cheerful grin. "There's nothing easier than that. The only hard part about it is getting to that carousel in the next three minutes. C'mon, Brody. It's not *that* big of a deal. Just go and get it over with so I still have enough time to hit the arcade before the show choir concert. I've got twenty bucks burnin' a hole in my pocket along with some killer moves for the dance game."

With only three minutes to get to the carousel, it wasn't like I even had time to argue anymore. But to be honest, I didn't want to argue. Solving this case and figuring out who was behind the text messages would help make Glitch a fully formed team again, and that thought alone made the hairs on my arm stand at attention.

Maddie was already up from her seat, smiling at me.

"Fiiiine," I fake-sighed as I joined Maddie.

We had only walked a few feet when Linus said my name. "Brody?"

I turned.

Linus tightened the kind of smile that said he was glad I was helping. "Thanks."

I don't know why, but like some kind of 1950's cool guy with a leather jacket, I pointed my fingers at him and made a "chk chk" sound with my cheek.

Maddie and I were out of the food court and moving faster than the mall walkers that exercised there everyday. Three minutes wasn't a long time, but it was long enough that we didn't have to fully sprint to the carousel.

"Linus has got a lot on his plate right now," Maddie said. "You know he's not normally like that."

"I know," I said, "but he could try to be *kind* of cool."

"I mean, you know what he's going through, right?" Maddie asked, and then explained as if I hadn't been around for awhile. "After Cob was booted from Glitch, Linus was the only one qualified to take control, but you saw what happened after he did that. Nearly everyone in Glitch quit because of it."

"They didn't quit because Linus was in command," I said. "They quit because Cob *wasn't* anymore. He had a lot of faithful agents working for him."

"Right," Maddie said. "But Linus is really struggling with it. Even though it wasn't personal, he's taking it personally. I think he's trying to prove himself with all this. This whole thing – the text messages and all – is his first real case, and I bet he'll be crushed if he botches it. Plus you know that we're technically not even a real agency anymore, right? We're pretty much operating on our own now."

"Still," I said. "He could be a little nicer about it."

"True. He might be overdoing it a bit." Maddie looked at me. "We all could be better leaders, Brody. I think Linus just needs a little more experience, and if taking a silly selfie is what's going to help him, then I don't think there's any harm in that."

Maddie was right. Linus was under a lot of pressure. Maybe all he needed was for someone to believe in him.

"He wants to be a better leader for Glitch," Maddie paused. "I want that for him too, but he's still got a lot to learn."

I nodded, not like I was answering, "yes," but that I understood what she was saying. I'm pretty sure my mouth was open and everything.

"Linus is like the tree trunk of Glitch," Maddie said. "And we're all the branches. As the trunk, Linus just needs to learn how to grow his roots."

"Or else all the branches will die," I said.

"Right," Maddie admitted, crinkling her nose. "Maybe that wasn't the best analogy."

"Ya think?" I grunted.

"We're here," Maddie said, stopping in place.

The small carousel was just outside one of the trendier clothing stores. There wasn't anyone on it, which made taking a selfie with it in the background a piece of cake. Or a piece of *carousel* cake, right? Wait, no... that's... nevermind.

Maddie held out her phone and nuzzled her face against my mine. I couldn't complain.

After snapping a photo, she brought up her profile and posted the picture on her wall. Then she handed me her phone.

"Nice shot, huh?" she asked, beaming with a smile.

"Totes," I said.

And then I noticed the other pictures on her timeline. They were all selfies of another girl in the school named Regina Roper.

"Regina's really into selfies, huh?" I asked, handing

Maddie's phone back to her.

"Right?" Maddie replied. "She posts at least a few *dozen* a day, and they're all the exact same shot at the exact same angle of the exact same kissy face."

I chuckled.

"Did you know she nicknamed herself '*Duckface, Queen of all Selfies*'?" Maddie added. "I think it'll even say that under her name in the yearbook."

"She seems to want everyone to know what she's up to at all times," I said.

Maddie agreed. "She's one of *those* people. She's like a kid splashing wildly in a pool, begging for everyone to look at her."

"Nice," I said. "My timeline is *flooded* with her selfies too, along with all kinds of hashtags."

You know what a hashtag is? It's when someone puts

this mark "#" in front of a word or a phrase. That way, people searching the Internet for posts about specific topics can find them easier.

"And they're all different!" Maddie said, annoyed. "Hashtag, *sunny day!* Hashtag, *soaking it in!* Hashtag, *love!* Hashtag, *cookies forever!* Hashtag, *heart!* Hashtag, *money* does *buy happiness!*"

"When I grow up," I said, "I'm gonna open an all day breakfast buffet called Scrambled Eggs and Hashtags. It's gonna be delicious!"

Maddie looked at me like she was waiting for the punch line. "Oh," she said. "I thought you were gonna say more."

"Uh, no," I said sheepishly, and then changed the subject back to Regina. "So yeah, she's got money too. Not that there's anything wrong with that, but she definitely likes everyone knowing. She always seems to have loads of cash."

"Maybe she's got a job?" Maddie suggested.

"Yeah, right," I said. "At our age?"

Maddie's phone buzzed.

"It's Linus," she said. "He wanted to tell us that we're doing a great job."

"At least he's being encouraging," I said.

"It's probably the same reason that he had back at the school," Maddie explained. "If we play along, it'll give K-pop and him a chance to try and figure out why these texts are getting sent in the first place."

"It's not a *bad* plan," I said. "It's just more of a '*wait-and-see*' plan."

"I'm just happy that there *is* a plan," Maddie said honestly. "Oh, look," she continued. "Regina just posted another selfie. This time she actually hashtagged the word *duckface*."

I studied the picture of Regina. "You know, it's eerie how alike you two look."

"Huh?" Maddie asked, gaping at the picture.

I went on. "Like, you two could be twins. Seriously, look at that. If you didn't tell me this *wasn't* you, I'd totally think it was."

Maddie huffed and looked away. She was uncomfortable with it, but seriously, Regina and Maddie looked like they could be *twins*. They looked so alike that it was kind of creepin' me out.

Again, Maddie's phone buzzed, but this time twice in a row.

"It's a picture of the pretzel shop on the second floor," Maddie said. "The second text says we have two minutes to get there."

"Guess that means we got two minutes to get there," I said.

"Ya think?" Maddie joked, and then randomly followed with, "Did you know Linus has an older brother?"

"Uh," I said. "No, I didn't."

"Yeah," Maddie said. "He's already graduated from high school. He's, like, nineteen-years-old or something."

I wasn't sure why Maddie felt like telling me this. "Okay," I said. "That's cool, I guess, but what's that have to do with us?"

Maddie curled her lip into a smile. "Because you're about to meet him."

With only two minutes to meet our selfie deadline, we had to half jog through the mall. The pretzel shop was on the second floor, and taking the elevator would've eaten up too much of what time we *didn't* have.

We decided to run to the part of the mall with the escalators and staircase, but when we got there, we were met by two of the mall security guards.

The taller of the security guards held his open hand out, stopping us in our tracks. "Escalator's closed, kiddos."

Maddie leaned over. "But that kid's on them," she said, upset and pointing at the kid halfway between floors on the escalator.

He was just walking in place at the same pace that the escalator was moving, not moving up or down, staying in the exact same spot between floors.

"Kid's been up there for about thirty minutes now," the security guard explained, clearly flustered.

"So get him off already," Maddie said, folding her arms.

The security guard arched an eyebrow. "No way, ma'am," he said. "We're not allowed to touch any citizens. It's strictly against mall policy to do so. We just have to wait here until he tires out."

Maddie's face tensed up. "That's crazy! Just get the kid off the escalator so other people can use it!"

"It's against policy to use force," the security guard said, shaking his head.

Maddie stepped aside and shouted, "Get off the escalator, bro! This isn't your home! It's not a playground for you to mess around in!"

The kid acted like he didn't even hear her, as he kept his perfect pace.

"You could use the staircase *next* to the escalator, or the elevator down the hall," the security guard said.

"Whatever," Maddie replied, as she took to the carpeted stairs next to the escalator. "C'mon, Brody. We don't have time for this."

I shrugged my shoulders at the security guard and followed Maddie up the stairs, passing the kid who was walking in place. Maddie didn't say anything to him, which was probably a good thing.

Up on the second floor, we jogged a little faster after Maddie glanced at the timer on her phone.

After rounding the bend, I could see the pretzel shop ahead of us. It was a small shop that was bright yellow and blue that looked out over the food court on the first floor.

I could see Linus, K-pop, and Janky still sitting at the table down below. Linus pointed up. K-pop and Janky turned in the chairs and waved to us.

K-pop brought her fists up and bobbed her shoulders back and forth. Then she tapped at an invisible watch on her wrist, reminding me that she still wanted to play that dance game at the arcade.

Maddie stopped right outside the pretzel shop, which was called "The Pretzel Palace." For the second time, she held out her cell phone and leaned into me, snapping another photo.

After posting it online, she let out a slow sigh.

"Welcome to the Pretzel Palace," the employee said with an accent I wasn't able to place, behind the counter of the shop. "Can I interest you in a pepperoni pretzel? Or perhaps a cinnamon pretzel? Or maybe a delightfully simple pretzel with only salt?"

I turned, facing the employee, surprised to see an older version of Linus, but with longer, flatter hair, staring back at me with eyes half shut. This must've been what Maddie meant when she said I was about to meet Linus's older brother. He had this soul patch thing goin' on too. It's like, hey, I want facial hair, but not a beard or a mustache. How 'bout something just to keep that spot below my lower lip warm?

"Hey, Teddy," Maddie said.

HOW MAY I HELP YOU?

TEDDY

2 YEARS OF SERVICE

The employee turned his body slightly to face her, like his neck wasn't able to turn at all. "Ahhh, yes, Maddie," he said in the same weird accent.

I couldn't tell what kind of an accent he had. It sounded familiar, but not so obvious. It was kind of driving me crazy.

"*There* is a face I haven't seen in some time," Teddy said slowly, like an old wise man remembering something from his past.

"How's business? Twisted, I hope," Maddie said, leaning against The Pretzel Palace's counter.

"Business is *good. Gooooooood*," Teddy drawled, his eyes still half shut. He took a deep breath through his nose. "The pretzels, this time of day, are *particularly* delectable. Is

58

that the right word? Delectable?" he asked, slowly over-pronouncing the word "delectable."

It took me a moment to realize that Teddy had asked *me* the question.

I tried to hold back a laugh, but wasn't able to. "I think? I guess that means they taste good?"

Teddy nodded slowly, or at least I *think* he nodded slowly. He still wasn't moving his neck. He kind of wobbled to and fro with his entire upper body. "Yes, yes," he said. "Delectable. It's as if the pretzels were tied in knots by the angels above, and hand delivered to this very palace… The Pretzel Palace."

I raised an eyebrow at Maddie. "What's happening? What is this? Is he speaking in some kind of code or something?"

Maddie smiled back. "No, Teddy just *really* loves his job."

Teddy smiled. "Yes, I certainly do. May I interest you in a garlic pretzel? Or perhaps one of our signature jalapeno cheese pretzels? The jalapenos are fresh this time of year. Yes," he continued in his weird accent. "It's quite the time for… wait for it… *pretzels*."

I leaned closer to Maddie. "What kind of accent is that?"

Maddie giggled. "It's fake," she explained. "He's just being a nerd. Teddy is a pretty cool dude, but he can be pretty weird sometimes."

Just like before, Teddy wobbled to and fro, as if he were nodding with his whole body. "Because the world needs more weird," he said, this time without the accent. "My job is boring. You're literally the first people to talk to me today. Wait, that's not true. I sold a pretzel to a girl a little bit ago."

"You've sold *one* pretzel today?" I asked.

"Pfft," Teddy puffed. "And she spent more time taking

59

pictures of the pretzel instead of eating it! Such amazing *explosions* of flavor when they're fresh, and she just... took *pictures* of it! You know how frustrating that is? It's like when someone puts milk in their bowl *before* their cereal!"

Maddie and I laughed.

Teddy sighed, and then spoke again. "How's my little bro?"

Maddie shrugged. "Stressed."

"Sixth grade problems can be real doozers," Teddy sighed. I think it was sarcastic, because he added, "I remember stressing out between tacos or pizza for lunch."

"Right?" I asked, and then immediately realized he *was* being sarcastic.

Maddie giggled again, covering her mouth with her hands.

"Well, tell my baby bro to stop by," Teddy said. "I can see him down in the food court. Tell him if he doesn't come up here before school's out, I'll embarrass the tar out of him."

"Will do," Maddie said as she turned around.

After saying bye to Teddy, I met Maddie at the bend in the corner.

"Teddy seems like a cool guy," I said.

"He is," she said. "Most of the time."

I laughed. "Well, that's all older brothers, isn't it?"

Maddie shrugged her shoulders and pulled her phone out of her pocket again. She clicked the home button and started sliding her finger across the screen.

But before she could unlock her phone, someone jumped out from behind her and snatched it out of her hands.

"Hey!" she shouted, reaching for her cell phone, but it was too far from her.

The boy with the phone spun in a circle, holding it out like he was taunting her. It was Jake, but his wolf pack was

nowhere to be—

At that moment, a bunch of boys snarling like wolves appeared from around the corner.

"Give it back!" Maddie said through her teeth.

"Tell me why," Jake sputtered.

"Uh, because it's mine?" Maddie said sarcastically.

"I don't see your name on it," Jake said, clicking the top button. The screen woke up from its sleep, displaying Maddie's picture along with her name at the top. "Oh, wait, there it is."

"Right," Maddie said, reaching for her phone. "Now give it back."

Jake pulled the phone away, holding it higher in the air like he was playing some kind of game of keep away, which was actually exactly what he was doing. "What's the magic word?"

"Does the magic word sound like a super loud scream?" Maddie asked. "Because I think a super loud scream will get enough attention that you'll *have* to give it back."

The rest of Jake's wolf pack formed a large circle around Maddie and me.

"C'mon, man," I said. "You're really gonna do this?"

"Just like you really burned the football team with your sign, back at the school?" Jake said. "Maybe I'll just take this phone as your way of making things right."

"That's not even *my* phone," I said.

A buzzing sound came from Maddie's cell phone. Jake lowered it from over his head and swiped his finger across the screen. He stared at it like a confused llama, trying to figure out exactly what he was looking at.

"Hey!" Maddie said. "Don't look at my message!"

Jake leaned backward, but continued peering at the cell phone. "Why did Linus forward you a picture of the Silver Dollar Fountain?"

Our next location.

Maddie straightened her posture. "What else is in the text? Does it say anything else?"

Jake blinked, looking back at Maddie. "One minute?" he said, raising his voice like he was still asking her why it would say that.

Maddie took Jake's moment of distraction and grabbed her cell phone out of his hand. Without waiting another second, she sidestepped the quarterback of the football team, totally dodging the rest of the wolf pack too as they reached out for her. Seriously, maybe Maddie should try out for the team.

"Brody!" she shouted over her shoulder. "One minute to get to the fountain! Go!"

While the wolf pack was trying to figure out how Maddie had so easily gotten past them, I took off running in the opposite direction, toward the staircase that led to the first floor.

Maddie was running *away* from the stairs, which meant she was going for the elevator.

I heard Jake grunt out of frustration, and then say, "Don't let him get away! He still owes us for the sign he wore!"

The pitter-patter of footsteps followed Jake's command, except it wasn't really a pitter-patter sound. It was more of a stomping noise.

Around the bend, I slowed when I saw the security guards that were watching the boy on the escalator. He still hadn't moved from his spot at the center of the escalator even though he was walking.

Holding my breath so I wouldn't sound like I had just finished a shuttle run, I quickly passed the security guards and walked down the steps at an irresponsibly fast speed for stairs.

Jake and his wolf pack were right behind me, trying to keep themselves from looking like they were part of a chase too, but with how distracted the security guards were, I don't think it mattered.

At the bottom of the steps, I cut a sharp left turn to head for the part of the mall with the Silver Dollar Fountain. Maddie was still running on the second floor. I could see her from where I was down below.

But before I could take off, one of the kids from the wolf pack grabbed my shirt, pulling me backward.

At the same time, a loud bell clanged right next to us. It was enough to scare the boy into loosening his grip on my clothing. I pulled forward, just enough to get away from the kid, but had to stop in my tracks to allow the kiddy train to drive by.

The bell was from the conductor of the train.

The boy who grabbed me, reached out again, but this time, I jumped forward, grabbing onto the back of the train as the caboose drove by.

The two bicycles that followed the train had to skid to a stop. The horse masks on the handlebars of both bikes wobbled back and forth, almost falling off.

The train wasn't driving fast, but it was still quick enough that I watched Jake's wolf pack stop their chase. Jake's face was red as his chest heaved up and down.

The two guys riding their horse bikes tried to confront Jake and his wolf pack about dangerously getting in the way, but in doing so, set their bicycles on the ground, unguarded.

Jake didn't waste any time. He scooped one of the bikes off the ground and pedaled away before anyone could stop him. Another one of the kids from his wolf pack did the same.

And there I was, hanging onto the caboose of a

miniature train driving through the mall while two kids on bicycles disguised as horses rode after me. It was like I was part of one of those silent western movies. The funky piano music playing over the mall's speaker system pretty much sold the whole scene.

It was easily one of the weirdest things that's happened in my life.

Jake and his buddy were closing the gap that separated us. They were standing while pumping the pedals of the bike so they could gain speed.

I looked down the front of the train, at the conductor who obviously didn't notice an extra passenger on his ride.

There were a few girls from school sitting in their carts, enjoying the view of the mall as they took pics of each other with their cell phones.

Jake was close enough that I could hear him huffing and puffing behind me.

Not wanting to waste another second, I grabbed the top of the caboose and hoisted myself up, so I was laying on my stomach.

Just then, the train turned the corner of the mall and down a small ramp. My body slid forward on the caboose, but at the bottom of the ramp the train turned again, and I was unable to keep myself from sliding off the side.

My fingers scraped the wood of the train until I caught the small window of the next cart, keeping myself from rolling to a painful end on the floor below.

Jake and his buddy slammed their bike pedals backward, skidding sideways at the ramp, keeping their bikes from toppling over.

Pulling myself back onto the top of the cart, I looked ahead to see where we were. The woman handing out samples at the vat of gazpacho stared at me as the train flew by at a staggering half mile an hour.

That meant we were back at the food court, and that the Silver Dollar Fountain was still several stores away… and in the opposite direction. I wasn't sure how in the heck I was going to make it there on time if I wasn't already late.

"Get off that train!" shouted Jake, suddenly appearing at my side and kicking his foot out at me.

I slid down the other side of the cart, dodging his kicks, but his wolf pack buddy was already on that side throwing kicks of his own.

I braced myself, squeezing my eyes shut for what was sure to be a painful boot to my butt when all of a sudden, things went pitch black.

"Great," I said to nobody. "I just died, didn't I?"

But when I opened my eyes, I realized that the train had

just entered a small cardboard tunnel that had been built just for the ride.

The light at the other end was coming up fast though, and I didn't feel like getting my butt kicked by Jake, so I hopped off in the dark tunnel. Don't worry; the train ride was seriously moving slower than a sloth on a lazy Sunday... that's a term, right?

I sprinted out of the back of the tunnel. Jake and his buddy were at the other end, waiting for the caboose to exit so they could catch me. Too bad I'd be halfway to the Silver Dollar Fountain before they realize I'd gotten away.

Finally, I had turned the last corner of the mall and reached the Silver Dollar Fountain. Since I wasn't keeping track of the clock, I had no idea if I made it on time or not.

Maddie was already there, tapping furiously at her cell phone with her thumbs.

"Did you post it?" I asked, catching my breath.

"Like, a couple *minutes* ago," Maddie said annoyed, staring at her cell phone. "I got here on time, but where were you?"

"Jake and his friends were after me!" I said, taking a seat on the edge of the fountain. The gold and silver colors reflected off Maddie's face like a kind of royal camouflage. "You have no idea what kind of strange chase I just got away from."

"Well, you're still late," Maddie said. "But it's cool because *I* wasn't."

Maddie's phone buzzed in her hands again. She stared at the little green box on her screen that had the number one in it, telling her she had a new message. I could tell she didn't want to read it, but she slid her finger across the screen.

She read slowly, aloud, and with a monotone voice. "It

was supposed to be both of you…"

"Uh-oh," I whispered.

Maddie and I looked at all the kids around the fountain, trying to see if the person at the other end of the texts was around and watching us, but it was impossible. There were just too many other mall shoppers.

We both sat on the edge of the fountain, wondering what was about to happen, if anything at all.

I was beginning to get my hopes up that it was all just some kind of lame-o prank, but that hope was crushed into dust pretty much instantly.

A smell, an *awful* smell, filled my nose. Maddie smelled it too, as did everyone else around us.

Mall shoppers stopped walking, and looked around, cringing their noses at the sudden blast of perfume that was in the air.

The smell wasn't putrid or nasty, like garbage or a skunk or anything, but was kind of the opposite, like it *could've* been pleasant if it wasn't so strong. It smelled like my parent's bathroom in the morning after they've gotten ready for work. Like a mixture of my mom's perfume and my dad's cologne.

Take that smell and times it by a billion. That's what was in the air around us.

It was strong enough that my eyes watered. "Where is that coming from?" I asked, pinching my nose shut.

Maddie splashed her hand in the water of the fountain, and then whipped it back and forth so it was mostly dry. Then she lifted her hand toward her face, but flinched before it even got close. "It's the water in the fountain!" she said. "Someone must've dumped a gallon of perfume into the fountain!"

"Why is someone doing this?" I asked, fully knowing Maddie didn't know the answer either.

Maddie and I just stared at each other, speechless, as the rest of the shoppers around us frantically left the area. Mother's clung to their children. Shop owners stood in their entrances. It was bonkers. Complete and total chaos.

Twenty minutes later, we were back with our friends in the food court. I had bought a cinnamon bun and was holding it close to my nose, trying to bring my sense of smell back from the nasty fountain water.

"Barf," K-pop said. "I wasn't even *near* the fountain, but that smell is in my mouth."

"Did you see anyone that looked suspicious?" Linus asked.

"Did *you?*" Maddie snipped angrily. Then she shut her

eyes. "Sorry. I didn't mean that. No. I didn't see anyone suspicious or near the fountain or anything."

"Where was Christmas?" I asked.

"He hasn't moved from his spot at that table back there," K-pop said, nodding her head in his direction. "He also hasn't touched his phone at all."

"Fine," I said. "Then let's just assume he's not the one behind this. Who does that leave?"

"Beats me," K-pop replied. "If it's not him, it could be anyone."

"We only had *one* minute!" Maddie said, frustrated.

"But even with the one minute, *you* still made it on time!" I said, taking a bite from my cinnamon roll, which tasted like perfume. I'm pretty sure I looked like a toddler when I scraped the top of my tongue against my upper teeth, letting the bite fall from my mouth and back onto the plate.

"Sick, man," K-pop whispered in disgust. "Manners, Brody. Manners."

Janky didn't say anything. He was sitting back in his chair, playing with a small red balloon, rolling it around in his hands.

Linus slapped his palm on the table at the thought of an idea. "We should go back to the fountain and look around for clues!"

"Except that part of the mall is shut down for the rest of the day," Maddie said. "Even the stores over there have been closed until the smell is gone. That section might be out for days. I guarantee this is a big enough deal that it's on the news tonight."

Janky's eyebrows raised. "You think they'll bring cameras?"

"Probably," Maddie said.

"Sweet," Janky said, pumping his fist. "Maybe I can get

on TV!"

"Get back in the game!" Linus said to Janky.

"What about you?" Maddie asked, annoyed that Linus had scolded Janky. "We've been running around the mall while you guys have done what? Sit here eating snacks?"

K-pop came to Linus's defense. She pulled out several sheets of paper. "No," she said. "As a matter of fact, we printed all the pictures and text messages from our mystery villain so we could study them at the same time. Trust me, I'd *rather* be at the arcade dancing my stress away, but I'm stuck here looking for clues like I'm part of some sort of mystery team that drives around in a van, and has a big brown dog that's afraid of *everything*." The words were flying out of K-pop's mouth as she grew more frustrated. *"What's up with that, dog? Why're you such a scaredy-cat? Maybe you shouldn't have joined their team if you can't look at your own reflection!"*

We all let K-pop take a second to calm herself.

"Sorry, guys," K-pop said. "I'm good now. It's not you guys, it's just… it's that *dog*. That's all. Foolish dog."

Maddie slid the printed pictures out on the table. "Where'd you guys find a printer?"

"We used the printer at the Pretzel Palace," Linus said, and then turned to look at me. "My brother works there."

"I know. I met him earlier," I said. "He told us he'd embarrass you if you didn't say hi to him, so I guess it's good that you went up there."

Linus shut his eyes halfway and spoke in a lower voice, mocking his brother. "The pretzels… are del-*ect*-able."

I snorted out a laugh. "Geez, that's, like, his thing, huh? Delectable pretzels."

"Dude, you have no idea," Linus said. "Teddy loves those pretzels *so much*. Like, he would marry them if it was

71

possible. He was *angry* that the only pretzel he sold today was to a girl who just took pictures of it."

I laughed again. "He told us that when we were up there!"

Maddie tapped at a sheet of paper on the table. "So here's the first text from the school," she said, and then waved her hand over the rest of the papers. "And here are all the pictures and texts afterward."

K-pop scanned the area around us. "So we're just gonna do this out in the open then?"

"It's not like we have a choice," Maddie said, studying the printouts. Her finger jabbed at each sheet of paper as she spoke. "The text at the school. The picture of the carousel. The picture of the pretzel shop on the second floor. And then a picture of the fountain. Each picture we got gave us less time to post a selfie at them."

"We only had a minute to get from The Pretzel Palace to the Silver Dollar Fountain," I added. "Sixty seconds to get from a spot on the second floor to the other end of the mall on the first floor. Even if I bolted, I would barely make that."

"But Maddie did it," Linus said proudly.

"Not like it mattered!" Maddie said. "It was like they *wanted* us to fail."

I sat back, feeling my stomach twist. "What if they did?"

Everyone at the table looked up at me.

"What if they wanted to dump the perfume in the fountain anyway?" I said. "I mean, Maddie made it on time and posted a selfie. We never had instructions to get there together, so she technically passed the challenge. There weren't any other rules to the game besides getting to those places and taking a pic. But the perfume was still set free."

"That would mean that all your running around was for nothing," Linus said, scratching at his chin. "But…"

"Exactly!" I said, pointing at our leader. "Why would we be going after all these selfies for nothing? It's a distraction! It's gotta be!"

"Wait, wait, wait," Janky said, rubbing his forehead. "Start over. This is all hurting my brain bank. I can *feel* the wrinkles in my brain smoothing out because of this."

"Okay, keep up," I said, jabbing the table with my finger. "Linus has been getting text messages demanding that we do something."

"Right," Janky said.

"We've been playing along to give you guys time to figure out who it is," I continued, jabbing again at the table.

"Okay," K-pop said. "Which we haven't done yet."

"So while we're chasing these text messages, this person planned on dumping perfume into the fountain all along," I said.

"Then why wouldn't they just skip all the games and dump the perfume to begin with?" Janky asked. "It's a lot of trouble to get us involved."

"To distract us!" I said, snapping my fingers.

"But to distract us from what?" Maddie asked. "What else is going on that would need a distraction?"

"I don't know," I said quietly. "I haven't gotten to that part yet."

Maddie groaned, folding her arms and leaning back in her chair. She took out her cell phone and starting scrolling through her online profile like she was done for the day.

We all sat quietly, staring at all the pictures Linus printed out, trying to make sense of the most confusing case we've ever had.

Maddie let out a laugh like a horse. "Regina," she said. "Regina is the one who took pictures of the pretzel. Hashtag, *fried bread*. Hashtag, *foodie*. Hashtag, *weirdo employee*."

"Hey," Linus said defensively. "That's my brother!"

"Regina's the girl who threw that roll at you back at school," K-pop added.

"That was *her?*" I asked.

"The *soup* thickens," Janky said.

"Plot," K-pop corrected. "The *plot* thickens. Well, I guess you could say soup too. Nevermind. You're fine. The *soup* thickens... when adding milk."

"Regina's rich," Janky added.

"Is there something wrong with that?" K-pop asked.

"No, no," Janky said. "I mean, there are some kids in school who have nice clothes and stuff, but you know it's all from their parents. I meant that *Regina's* rich. She seems to have cash all the time, and isn't afraid to flaunt it."

"Now that you say that, I see it," Linus said. "Like she's got a job or something."

Janky grinned. "Yes! Like she's got a job," he repeated.

Maddie flicked her thumb, scrolling through her timeline. "Man, Regina's posted a billion selfies at the mall already. We've only been here for, like, thirty minutes."

Janky smiled. "You and Regina look like twins."

"Whatever," Maddie said, half smiling. "You and Brody just need to get your eyes checked."

I leaned closer to see Maddie's phone. "Oh, look! There she is by the fountain!" I said, watching Maddie's timeline slow to a stop. "And that's her by the carousel too..."

Scattered throughout Regina's pictures, were her selfies at the three locations we had been commanded to be at by our mystery villain.

Maddie didn't move her head, but her eyes looked at me. "Look at the timestamp."

"1:10 PM," I read aloud. The picture was of Regina at the carousel."

Maddie tapped one of the printed picture messages from Linus's phone. She put her finger by the timestamp of his text. "1:11 PM," she said.

The picture of her selfie with the pretzel had a timestamp of 1:15 PM. And Linus had gotten his message at 1:16 PM. The same thing happened with the fountain. One minute after Regina posted a selfie, Linus had gotten a message with a picture of the fountain.

"Whoa," Janky said.

"Hold on," K-pop said. "So Regina just happened to be in those places around the same time. It could be a terrible coincidence and nothing else. Let's not get out the pitchforks just yet."

"Should we confront Regina?" I asked, looking to Linus to give some kind of advice.

"No," he said spinning his cell phone on the table, "because if it's Regina, we don't want her to know that we're onto her."

"Then how do we figure out if it's her?" Maddie asked.

K-pop snatched Linus's phone off the table.

"Hey!" Linus said.

But K-pop was already tapping her thumbs on his screen.

"What're you doing?" he asked.

"Something that didn't occur to me earlier," K-pop said, showing us the screen of his phone. She had brought up the unknown number and had somehow dialed it back. "Sometimes when you get an unknown number, you can automatically call it back. If it works, then your phone will show the number it's calling even though it was blocked when it called you."

We watched as K-pop let the mystery number ring once, and then she immediately hung up. She held the phone out for

75

us to see, showing us that it worked. There was a ten-digit phone number on the screen.

Then K-pop took Maddie's phone from her hand. "Since Linus was just forwarding those texts to you," K-pop said to Maddie, "she won't recognize *your* phone number."

"Okaaaay," Maddie said, as K-pop typed a text message to the new phone number from Maddie's cell phone. "What're you gonna do? Just ask if that's Regina's number? Pretty sure that'll sound suspicious."

"Nope," K-pop said, setting the phone down so we could all watch. "I'm gonna make it look like an *accidental* text."

"Ha," Janky laughed. "Like a butt dial? Except for it's a butt text!"

"No," K-pop said flatly. "Not like that."

The message K-pop typed was, *"Hey, where u at? Gotta be at work in five mins. U still giving me a ride?"*

We all waited patiently after K-pop hit "send," staring at Maddie's phone.

At long last, the number responded. *"Sry. U got the wrong number."*

K-pop didn't flinch. She knew exactly how to reply. *"Quit playin, dork! If I'm late again, they'll fire me!"*

Maddie's phone buzzed with another reply. *"U got the wrong number. Stop texting me."*

K-pop typed again, and super fast too. *"Amber? This isn't funny. Imma be in serious trouble if I'm late."*

"U have the wrong number. My name is Regina. Not Amber."

"Boom!" K-pop said, slapping the table. "It *is* Regina's phone."

I sunk down in my seat. "What the heck? Why would she send us on those missions?"

"Because she's crazy," Maddie said, shrugging her shoulders. She looked at Linus. "So now what? Now that we know it's her, what do we do? We don't know *why* she's doing all this. We don't even know where she is!"

Linus's phone buzzed again. He slid his finger across the screen and smiled. "Oh, yes we do," he said, showing us the picture message he had gotten.

It was a picture of the toy store near the entrance of the mall with the words, "Ten minutes," underneath it.

"Ten minutes is a *long* time," I said.

"She's still playing?" Janky asked, confused. "Why?"

"Who cares?" Maddie replied. "Now that we know she posts selfies before sending Linus a message, we can easily catch her! We have the upper hand here!"

"That's great," K-pop said. "Janky and I can dress up

like you guys and make her think you're still going on these selfie missions. That way, you and Brody can try to get ahead of her!"

"Sounds good," Linus said. He looked at me. "You up for that?"

"Yup," I answered.

Linus continued as he scooped up the printed sheets of paper. "While you four are out in the field playing Regina's game and distracting her, I'm going to find a place to set up a base. I'll keep studying her texts and even her hashtags now. I'm pretty sure I can find a pattern in all this, which will tell us *exactly* what her end-game is. We're gonna do this, guys. We're gonna crack her code and save the day."

K-pop inhaled deeply and stretched out her back. "But save the day from what? *That's* the question."

Even though we all heard her question, nobody answered it because the truth was that we had no idea what Regina's reason was behind all the things she was doing.

But still, it felt good to know that Glitch was back on track. Regina might have been playing a game with us earlier, but now we were the ones in control, and whatever psycho plan she had was going to be stopped… hopefully.

A few minutes later, Maddie and I were standing outside the food court restrooms, waiting for K-pop and Janky to come out with their disguises. Linus had already disappeared to some secret location in the mall, which totally meant he was going to find a dark broom closet or something.

K-pop was the first out of the women's restroom, wearing a wig that looked like my hair, along with an entire outfit that was the same one I was wearing. I was a little surprised at how preppy I dressed and—wait a minute… K-pop was supposed to be *me?*

"Why are you me?" I asked K-pop.

K-pop chuckled, but before she could answer, Maddie spoke up.

"If you're him, then that means Janky's—" Maddie stopped midsentence.

"S'up, sugar?" Janky said as he walked out of the men's restroom, wearing a blonde wig.

I couldn't help but laugh at the sight of Janky. He looked like he had long flowing hair made of gold. It was a huge difference from how he normally looked. And because his head was so bright now, I totally noticed the patchy mustache he was also sporting.

"I don't call people sugar!" Maddie snipped. "Switch

wigs with K-pop right now!"

Janky twirled the fake yellow hair around his finger. "No way! This makes me feel pretty!"

"Yeah," K-pop snorted. "It makes him feel pretty! Don't you dare take that from him!"

"You don't think it shows too much forehead though, does it?" Janky asked.

"No, man!" I said, trying to comfort my friend. "If anything, it doesn't show *enough* forehead!"

"What's that supposed to mean?" Maddie squawked.

"I was joking!" I said through a laugh.

The whole thing was silly enough that we all LOL'd. Even Maddie.

"Whatever," Maddie said. "You're the one who's gotta take a selfie like that."

Janky smiled softly, turning his head and fluttering his eyelashes.

K-pop glanced at the time on Maddie's phone. Maddie had given K-pop her cell phone so she and Janky could post selfies to Maddie's wall.

Maddie and I still had my phone so we could try and follow Regina's selfie trail.

"C'mon, Janky," K-pop said. "We gotta get moving. We've only got about five minutes to get to the toy store and take a picture."

After K-pop and Janky left, I brought up Regina's profile. She had taken a few pictures with the toy store behind her, but had posted about ten selfies since then.

"Whoa," I said. "She's posting so much that I don't have a clue where she is."

"What's her last picture?" Maddie asked.

"A plate of egg rolls," I said.

"She's here in the food court?" Maddie said, stretching

80

her neck up.

"No, wait," I said. "She just posted again. This time there's a baby clothing store behind her."

"Sweet," Maddie said. "That means she's going down the west end of the mall."

I always forget which way east and west were so I always had to use that rhyme they taught us in kindergarten. Under my breath, I said, "Never eat shredded wheat…"

"Really?" Maddie asked with a smirk.

"What?" I said. "My dad still does it too!"

"I'm kidding," she said. "*Everyone* does it."

Maddie took the lead and walked out into the food court. Following behind her, I squinted to see as far ahead as I could, hoping to find Regina, but of course I didn't. These things were never that easy.

As I looked across the tables of the food court, I saw a bunch of kids from show choir setting up more stuff around the stage they were going to use for their performance.

A few of the kids were already wearing the costumes for the show. Purple robes made from heavy fabric hung off their bodies like they were shaolin monks or even better, Jedi masters.

The woman with the gazpacho samples was following some of them around, desperately trying to get them to take a sip of the cold soup. It made me shudder.

And then I accidentally made eye contact with Christmas. He was still at his table, surrounded by his goons in suits. He nodded his head once at me, holding up his Styrofoam cup as if he were toasting me.

I knew that we didn't have any evidence that Christmas was part of Regina's plan, but I couldn't help but feel as though he knew everything that was happening. The way he was sitting in the middle of his Suckerpunch agents just looked like he was patiently waiting for something to happen.

I nodded back at him, only because it was instinct to nod at someone who nods at me. And then I brought my attention back to Maddie who had gotten way ahead of me. I had to focus on finding Regina and get Christmas out of my mind. If he had *anything* to do with what was happening, then he wouldn't be sipping on a drink with such a smug look on his face.

I mean, right?

At the baby clothing store, Maddie and I stopped to sit on a bench, watching as all the shoppers walked by.

Maddie pointed up at the second floor. "Look," she said.

K-pop and Janky were hustling to get to a place that Regina wanted them to take a selfie at. Both of them had looks of joy as they sidestepped shoppers.

"At least *they're* having fun," I said as I scrolled through the timeline on my phone. Finally, I stopped at Regina's most recent selfie. "She's at that kiosk that sells all those sunglasses," I said to Maddie.

"Okay, well I don't want to play a game of just following her," Maddie said. "So let's try to get *ahead* of her and guess where she's *going* to be."

"The kiosk is by all those other kiosks around that indoor playground," I said.

"Which is also by the mall entrance," Maddie added as she hopped up from the bench. "Let's try to get there before she posts another picture of herself."

And again, I followed Maddie's lead as she sped down the mall, passing all the spots we had already covered from the first hour of being there.

Most of the students and teachers were in the food court, waiting for the show choir to finish setting up the props for their show.

Christmas was at a table surrounded by his Suckerpunch agents.

The lady with the gazpacho had a smile on her face as we walked by her *again*. Small drops of red soup had dried on her apron from when I spat it out at her earlier.

The bell from the mini-train echoed down the huge hallways of the mall, ringing somewhere out of view. The bikes disguised as horses most likely rode beside it.

The boy on the escalator still had his place perfectly set, at the center of the moving stairs. The security guards had put up yellow caution tape to keep people from getting on the escalators.

The scent of freshly cooked pretzels drifted down from the second floor as we passed the escalators, and I found myself craving a pretzel. The way Linus's older brother had talked about them made me really want one. Greasy knots of salted bread and cheese that tasted like plastic – *yum*.

And then, finally, the mall entrance was up ahead of us. Younger kids played on the indoor playground as their parents sat on the benches around it, just inside the front doors of the mall.

The kiosk with the sunglasses was to the far right of the playground, along with a bunch of other kiosks that sold random things – makeup, cell phone covers, strange jewelry with magnets. There was even a kiosk with pictures of hot tubs and showers. I guess if you ever want to buy a hot tub, just go to the mall and order one.

"Got her," Maddie said, grabbing my elbow.

Regina Roper was standing at the other end of the playground, looking out the glass doors of the mall entrance like she was waiting for someone.

"What do we do?" I asked.

Maddie blinked, staring at the ground as she thought. "I don't know," she admitted.

"I don't feel like running through the mall again," I said. "So let's not do anything to freak her out."

Maddie agreed. "But the second she sees us, she's gonna bolt. She knows *exactly* who she's been messing with all day. When we show up behind her, she's gonna freak out and try to escape. Everyone always does!"

"Then she needs something that'll keep her from running," I said.

"There's *nothing* to keep her from doing that," Maddie said.

Panic filled my thoughts. "What're we gonna do? She's here right now, but in about a second, she's gonna bounce and find another place to go!"

Maddie pointed back at Regina. "Maybe not…"

I looked at Regina, who was now standing next to one of the automatic doors as it slid open. Two adults walked through the door. A man in a business suit, and a woman wearing a fancy looking dress.

"Who's that?" I asked.

Maddie paused. "Regina's parents."

"Yes!" I said. "We need to get over there right now."

"I don't know," Maddie said.

"This is the perfect chance for us!" I explained. "With Regina's parents hovering around, there's no way she'll run!"

"Huh," Maddie grunted. "*Sounds* like a good idea, but what're you gonna say to her with her parents around? '*We know you're an evil villain plotting against us?*' We'll sound like *we're* crazy."

I turned back to Maddie, holding my arms out like "*whatever*," and said, "Then I won't say *that,* alright? Now come on. We'll just have a little talk with her."

Regina's voice was pretty clear as Maddie and I got closer. She was telling her parents all about her morning at school, and about the last hour of being at the mall. But the odd thing about the conversation was how shaky her voice sounded, like she was nervous about something.

Maddie and I huddled behind one of the giant turtle shells on the indoor playground, waiting for Regina and her parents to walk a little farther into the mall.

"Okay, genius," Maddie joked. "Now what? Should we shout at her from behind this turtle?"

"Noooo," I sang, wobbling my head and using mocking tone. "When they walk by, we'll casually stroll up behind them. Cool?"

Maddie huffed about it, but didn't argue.

Once Regina and her parents passed the turtle shell, Maddie and I snuck out of the indoor playground.

I wanted to yell Regina's name, but stopped when she

pulled out her cell phone again.

Huddling against her parents, Regina snapped a selfie of all three of them, with me in the background. She was still facing away from Maddie and me as she clicked a couple buttons on her phone.

Regina's shoulders jerked forward. She spun in place and stared at me with eyes as large as the moons of Jupiter. "Brody!" she wheezed.

Everything happened so quickly that I froze up too. "Regina!" I said without thinking.

Regina's parents stopped and looked as well. I'm sure Maddie was somewhere behind me but I had no idea where.

Then Regina's mom came forward with a concerned look on her face. The kind of look that wasn't angry or mad or sad or happy or *anything at all* even. The kind of look that was impossible to read. My parents were good at giving that look. I was about get scolded or about to get a pat on the back. I wasn't sure.

"Is this one of your friends?" Regina's mom asked.

Regina took a second to answer, but finally said, "Yep! Brody's a buddy of mine. We're buddies. And that's Maddie back there too. Good to see you guys!"

Regina's dad stayed back like he was a statue keeping watch.

Her mom spoke again as she smiled. "Oh, are the two of you in show choir also? You must be so excited for the performance today."

"Yeah, mom," Regina quickly answered for us. "They're in the show choir too."

"*Too?*" Maddie whispered to me.

Regina must've been able to read Maddie's lips because she instantly spoke again. "Mom, why don't you take dad down to the food court and get something to eat? I gotta catch up with these two friends of mine."

"Friends from the choir?" her mom asked.

Regina paused. "...friends from the choir," she repeated.

"Yes, of course, sweetie," her mom replied. She took her husbands elbow and they started for the food court. "We'll see you after your performance, honey! Good luck to all three of you!"

Once Regina's parents had walked far enough away, Regina turned to face Maddie and me, but she didn't say anything. Her eyes were fixed on the floor, staring at nothing. I expected her to start running, but she never did.

"We're not in show choir," Maddie said at last.

"I know," Regina said softly.

"Then why'd you tell your parents we were?"

Regina shrugged her shoulders.

"What just happened back there?" Maddie asked, confused.

"Nothing," Regina said. "It was just easier to tell my parents that instead of, y'know... everything else."

"You're finished," Maddie said. "You know that, don't you? This whole game you've been playing with us is over."

"And now you're gonna tell us exactly why you've been messing with us all day," I added.

Regina took a deep breath, and then looked up at me. Her lip quivered as her eyes grew wetter with tears.

"C'mon," I said, fully knowing that I was a sucker for a crying girl. "It's okay... there's no need for that..."

Maddie wasn't having any of it though. She folded her arms and planted her feet firmly in the ground. "A sob story isn't gonna help you right now, Regina. Tell us why you've been playing us!"

"It wasn't me!" Regina's voice cracked as she spoke. It was as if the volume knob on her voice cranked all the way up, and then broke off. "I don't know why I'm doing these things, okay?"

Maddie put her arms out, flustered. "What's that even mean? We know you were the one sending the texts! And the fact that you're crying right now pretty much tells us you know what we're talking about!"

"But I'm innocent! I really have nothing to do with this!" Regina said, and then she dropped the bomb. "It was Moss! It was Christopher Moss that told me to do all that to you guys! He's the one you want! Not me! He's the one who poured those bottles of perfume into the fountain!"

I was too floored to say anything. All this time, it was Christmas pulling the strings, not Regina.

"But *why?*" Maddie asked.

"I don't know!" Regina sniffled. She wiped her nose with the back of her hand, and then covered her face, crying even harder. "Please, my parents are here! Please don't say anything! I'll go to the principal after the show choir concert, okay? Will that make you happy?"

Regina was sobbing so loudly that it was hard to understand her. The other people in the mall were beginning to look. Even Maddie had grown uncomfortable and was starting to show that she felt sorry for Regina.

Maddie put her hand on Regina's shoulder, but in an awkward "*I'm not sure how to comfort you*" kind of way.

"Okay," Maddie said. "Just… stop crying already. Everybody's looking."

Regina snorted into her hands. "You guys are gonna be cool? You aren't gonna turn me in?"

I wasn't sure what Maddie wanted to do so I said

nothing.

"No," Maddie groaned. "Christopher made you do all that, and there wasn't any real harm done. So no, there's no reason to bust you for it."

Regina's eyes sparkled. "Oh, thank you! Thank you, thank you, thank you!"

"But this doesn't mean it's over," Maddie added. "Christopher wanted you to do all this, but we still don't know why. We're going to have to talk to him."

"Yes, of course!" Regina said, nodding quickly. "Of course you do! He's the one behind it all, not me. He's the one you have to get!"

Maddie and I didn't waste any more time with Regina. Standing beside a sobbing girl was awkward enough as it was, and the two of us didn't need the kind of attention she was bringing.

Maddie gave Regina a tissue to wipe her tears with, but allowed Regina to leave after that.

Even though the selfie game was finished, the mystery was still there. Why did Christmas use Regina for his plan? *What* was his plan? He'd been sitting in the food court the whole time we had been at the mall, so whatever he was doing didn't involve him getting his butt out of that chair.

The only thing I could even think of was that he was just spreading Glitch out even thinner by getting us to chase after someone for no reason at all. He knew Glitch was barely a secret agency anymore, and all he had to do was put a tiny bit of pressure on us to break the group apart.

If that's what he was up to, then Christopher Moss was seriously some kind of evil genius.

After getting a text from Linus telling us where he was, Maddie and I made our way back through the mall again. It was weird constantly going back and forth from one end of the shopping center to the other.

Normally, I never leave the arcade while my parents shop and stuff. Well, when my *mom* shops, and my dad finds a bench closest to the store she's in. It's kind of funny because there's always sixth graders staring at their phones, waiting for their parents to finish shopping, but my grown up dad does the exact same thing.

Sometimes I think that adults are just bigger versions of kids.

The text from Linus said he was in one of the maintenance closets on the second floor, near the Pretzel Palace. I totally knew he'd set up shop in a dark closet somewhere.

The closet was down a long hallway, and next to some restrooms. When we got to the door, Maddie and I stopped.

"Should we, like, have a secret knock or something?" I asked.

Maddie let out a puff of air through her nose, laughing. "Uh, no," she said, pushing down the metal handle of the door.

But as soon as she opened the door half an inch, someone on the other side pushed it back shut.

"Hey!" Maddie said.

"Who is it?" came Linus's voice from behind the oversized metal door.

"Who do you think?" Maddie snipped, and then sarcastically said, "It's Genghis Khan, and I'm here to conquer the maintenance closet! It's mine now so open the door! Gimme all your brooms!"

Linus's voice shouted behind the door again. "Yeah right! Genghis Khan died like a thousand years ago!"

"Is he kidding right now?" I asked. "Did he really just think you were trying to pass as *Genghis Khan*?"

91

Maddie shrugged her shoulders. "Linus, let us in already!" she said, pushing down on the handle and bumping into the door with her shoulder.

Linus let the door open an inch and stared at us through the crack. "What's the password?" he asked.

LINUS ...I THINK.

"What password?" Maddie said, frustrated. "You never gave us a password!"

Linus fell silent for a second as Maddie and I stared at each other.

Finally, the door swung open steadily. As soon as I saw Linus's face, I was blasted by a wall of hot air. It was as if he had just opened the door to a sweat lodge.

From somewhere in the room came a low rumbling sound like a machine struggling to stay alive somewhere. At various other parts of the large closet were short bursts of "pshh!" sounds, like something was being powered by a steam engine.

"Sorry 'bout that," Linus said, sweat dripping from his face. "Thought I gave you guys a password."

"Dude," Maddie said, stepping into the room. "It's gotta be over a hundred degrees in here!"

Linus wiped his forehead with the back of his hand. "Nah," he said. "It's not that hot. Besides, there wasn't anywhere else I could set up our base."

I didn't realize how little light was actually in the closet until I let the door shut behind me. We were standing in a room full of shadows and dull yellow glows from the single light bulb buzzing over our heads.

As I walked backward to see if there were any kind of vents I could open to get more air into the room, I found myself in the middle of a giant spider web made from strings of yarn.

At each point where the yarn turned, Linus had taped up a small sheet of paper that had a handwritten hashtag on it. There were easily dozens of those small slips of paper that were scattered throughout the room. Several other slip of paper were printed photos of random students from Buchanan.

"Linus," Maddie said, moving through the strings without touching them, like it was some kind of laser maze. "What have you been up to?"

Linus took the bottom of his shirt, pulled it up, and wiped the salty sweat off his face. With what I think sounded like a chuckle, he spoke. "I've figured it out, Maddie. It took me a little bit of time, but I've figured it out! The *code*... has been *cracked!* By *me!*"

"Ummmm," I hummed. "We've only been gone for, like, fifteen minutes."

Linus nodded rapidly like a bobblehead. "Uh-huh, uh-huh. I knew I didn't have much time so I had to work fast! Like, warp speed fast!"

"Except that Regina—" I started to say, but Linus interrupted me.

"Regina's plan is to *take over the world!*" Linus said, flicking one of the hashtagged slips of paper. "She posted this hashtag at the beginning of the day! You see it? It says hashtag, *beautiful sunrise*. Seems innocent, right?"

"Yeah," I said, watching the leader of Glitch go crazy.

"Wrong!" he said. "If I recall correctly, the sky was *cloudy* this morning, which could only mean that Regina was using that fake hashtag as a secret code, but let me ask you this – to *who*, Brody? *Who was Regina sending her coded message to?*"

I shrugged my shoulders because I couldn't quite form

any words with my mouth.

"Exactly!" Linus said. "It's the million dollar question that I was burnin' to find the answer to!" He spun in a circle to show us his web of hashtags. "The answer is Roxy! Regina was sending a secret message to Roxy Adams, one of the other sixth graders at Buchanan School. How do I know the message was to Roxy? Because Roxy's name means 'dawn,' and 'bright,' which is what Regina meant by *beautiful sunrise!*"

Maddie folded her arms, listening carefully.

"But *why* Roxy?" Linus asked as if he were speaking for us. Tiny beads of sweat jumped off his forehead and splattered on the concrete by his feet. "I'll tell you why! Because Roxy's her evil business partner! *And* because Roxy's uncle owns the butcher shop down the street from my house! Regina was getting Roxy's attention with her first hashtag of the day, basically telling her to get ready. The hashtag *after* that said, *'late TBT!'* It said *'late'* because today is Friday, and she posted something meant for yesterday!"

With his first finger, Linus tapped the photo that Regina had posted along with the 'late TBT' tag. It looked like a class picture of Regina, but much younger. She had a bright yellow shirt with some words printed on the front of it, but the photo was small enough that I couldn't read it from where I was standing.

Maddie nudged me with her elbow. While Linus was too distracted by his web of yarn, she made circles with her finger next to her noggin, letting me know that Linus was off his rocker.

Linus continued his descent into lunacy. "Hashtag, *late TBT.* Everyone knows TBT means 'Throwback Thursday' – a day when you're supposed to post really old pictures of yourself, but what if Regina meant '*Tiny Bacon Train*' instead?"

"Tiny. Bacon. Train," Maddie repeated.

I didn't say anything, but I wanted to call dibs on "Tiny Bacon Train" as a band name. I have a whole list of band names to go through when I actually start a band someday.

"So remember Roxy's uncle's butcher shop? Well, get this - that shop just happens to make a tiny bacon train to display in their windows during the holidays. It's bacon wrapped smokies hooked together and lined up on a track made of toothpicks," Linus said, taking a deep breath and smiling. "I know, right?" he then asked, nodding with a satisfied smile beaming across his face.

Maddie and I just stared back at him.

"Now if we take 'tiny bacon train' and rearrange the letters in it," Linus said so fast it sounded like a chipmunk, "then we get the phrase '*Baa Tic Ninny Ort*,' which *everyone* knows is Latin for '*The sun rises at midnight!*'"

"Pretty sure that's not Latin," Maddie said, shaking her head. "Pretty sure those are just nonsense words you made up."

But Linus didn't stop talking. "Now I *know* what you're thinking!"

"Do you?" Maddie asked sarcastically.

He pointed his finger at her. "But Linus," he said with a much deeper voice, "How can the sun rise at midnight? Well, the answer is that the sun is always rising somewhere on Earth when the clock strikes midnight!"

Maddie slumped her shoulders. "That's exactly what I was thinking," she said.

"So this thing that Regina is planning is going to happen when our clock strikes midnight!" Linus finally said. "But *what* is she planning? *World domination.* And how do I know?" he asked, walking back to the '*late TBT*' hashtag. He tapped on the photo that was attached to it. "Because in this photo – Regina's *kindergarten* class photo – she's wearing a bright yellow shirt that has the words, 'Future Ruler of the World,' printed on it."

Once Linus finished, he let himself rest against the door to the hallway, looking back and forth between Maddie and me, like he was waiting for one of us to call him brilliant. "Boom," he said proudly while catching his breath.

Maddie shot a look at me. Her eyes were wide, but her eyebrows were angled down like she was angry or something. It was the look of concern that our friend had officially driven himself crazy, trying to crack a code that didn't exist. Regina's hashtags were simply random words that explained what she was up to in her posts. They didn't mean anything at all.

"That's all a great theory," Maddie said, "but it's Christmas behind the whole thing. He's the one that got Regina to send us all those texts, and none of her hashtags mean a thing. They're just random words."

Linus's face twitched as he blinked hard. "No," he said, pointing at his magical web of crazy. "It's all because of the tiny bacon train! Roxy and her uncle's butcher shop!"

"Do you hear yourself?" Maddie asked, opening the door to the hallway so some fresh air would start pouring in. "You're saying that Regina is planning to take over the world at midnight because the tiny bacon train told you so!"

"I…" Linus said, taking a deep breath of crisp, clean air. "When you put it like that, then yeah, *maybe* it sounds a little crazy."

Linus came into the hallway, shielding his eyes from the bright fluorescent lights above. His sweat soaked shirt was hanging off his body, trying to pull him to the floor. He looked like a cave dweller that was seeing the sun for the first time in his life.

K-pop and Janky had rejoined us since Regina wasn't

sending any more texts to them. They had already taken their wigs off and looked normal again, but Janky was still rolling around the red water balloon in his hands.

"So Christmas is behind this?" Linus asked, rubbing his eyes. "Guess I'm not surprised. But why? What did Regina say?"

"She just said that Christmas was the one making her send us those texts," I said.

"He had to have a reason," Linus said.

"Probably just to mess with us," K-pop said. "Didn't he say that Suckerpunch was all about causing chaos? Like, that's the only reason it even exists as an agency?"

"Careful," Linus said. "We can't say that's the *only* reason. I just can't believe that any of those kids live to make life difficult for the other students at Buchanan. I'm sure they have a reason, we just don't know it."

"Christmas is a kid repeating the sixth grade," K-pop said. "Can you imagine having to go through that? All your friends would be in the next grade up, but still at the same school, while you were in a class full of kids you only kind of knew about from the year before. Ouch."

K-pop had a point. Christmas had always just been the "bad guy" to me. I had never actually thought about what kind of things he was going through himself.

It was only a year ago that Christmas was a member of Glitch. He *used* to be one of the good guys. If he was anything like the other members of our agency, he was probably a pretty cool kid, devoted to keeping Buchanan out of trouble.

And then, for one reason or another, he was told he'd have to repeat sixth grade, and because of that, had to remove himself from the agency.

I guess every villain had an origin story. Too bad his wasn't in a comic book I could read... maybe someday.

Linus scratched his head. "We need to get to Christmas," he said.

"And put him in detention for the rest of the year," Janky said, still playing with his red water balloon.

"Dude, what's up with the balloon?" I finally asked.

K-pop shut her eyes and groaned as if she was already annoyed by his answer.

"Bros," Janky said with a smile spreading wide on his face as he held up the small red balloon, presenting it to us. "And, uh… sisters," he added. "In every spy movie, there's always that one guy who creates doodads and gadgets for the spies to use when they're in the field."

"Right," I said. "Like laser watches and cars with rocket thrusters."

Janky snapped his fingers at me. "Exactly," he said. "Well, I'd like to be *that* guy in this agency. Glitch needs someone to craft cool trinkets and stuff so you guys can have tools to use when you're on a case or something."

"Get to the point, Janky," K-pop said, rubbing the bridge of her nose.

"Agents of Glitch," Janky said. "I present to you… the onion baked bean water balloon."

"…the what now?" Maddie asked after a brief moment of silenced confusion.

"It's a water balloon," Janky explained, "that's filled with cold baked beans. The onion kind."

K-pop chewed her lip. "That just makes me think that maybe you shouldn't be allowed near water balloons until you're older."

"Whatever!" Janky said. "The package said '*8 and up!*' That's totally me!"

"But… why beans?" I asked.

"Why not?" Janky replied. "The cool thing about those

99

agents in the movies is that they always seem to have just the right tool for whatever's happening to them."

"And a balloon filled with baked beans is somehow going to come in handy for one of us?" Maddie asked.

Linus chuckled, staring at the balloon. "I guess if the agent was at a picnic with a bunch of clowns, and someone was like, 'we're out of baked beans! Does anybody know where we can get baked beans delivered to the other end of the table without actually walking over there? *We need a way for someone to throw the beans into a pot from several feet away!*'"

Janky pouted angrily.

"Sorry, man," Linus said. "I'm just messing with ya. Every great spy doodad inventor has to start somewhere, right?"

Janky's face turned with excitement. "Yes! I got a million ideas! Like, I want to hide a cell phone on the inside of a banana! Or, like, headphones inside some English muffins! Or even use a watermelon to hold whatever disguise you'll need to use later!"

"You're just putting things inside of food!" K-pop said.

Janky didn't see the problem. "So?"

As Janky and K-pop continued to argue, Maddie walked to the end of the hallway and peeked her head out. "You know, Christmas is *right there* with the rest of his agents. They're all even in the exact same spots around Christmas as they were down below. They must have assigned seating."

"What?" Janky asked. "All afternoon, he's been in the food court! Now he's up here?"

"He's looking over the edge of the railing," Maddie explained. "Maybe he wanted a better view of the show choir concert."

"His agents are around to protect him," Linus said.

"They wouldn't let us get within twenty feet of the kid."

Janky leaned over to get a better view of Christmas and the Suckerpunch agents. "What do you mean? Like, they'll start a fight or something?"

"No," Linus said. "Even smart villains know that fighting is the most useless way to do anything. If those agents threw out punches, then adults would be all over them in a heartbeat. Nope. Those guys'll likely just cause a scene to embarrass us or distract us while Christmas got away."

"That's if he sees any of you guys," Maddie said. "He's got a super crush on me, so he'd totes let me sit at the table with him, but there's no way I'm gonna do that."

I'm not sure why, but I felt a little uneasy about hearing that Christmas had a crush on Maddie. "He does?"

"Oh, yeah," she said. "He's not a creep about it though, so I guess that's good."

"Maddie's right," Linus said. "If he sees me, K-pop, or Janky walk near him, his agents will be right on top of it. Except for Maddie... and *you*," Linus said from behind me as I glanced out the hall at Christmas, careful so he didn't see me.

Or you? Was that what Linus said? Who was he talking about?

When I turned around, I had my answer. Everyone on the team was looking at me.

"He wanted you to join Suckerpunch," Linus said. "That's what you told us. If he wanted you to join, I bet he'd be cool with talking to you still."

I laughed. "Yeah, right," I said. "If I had a bucket list, that's something that *wouldn't* be on it – talking to Christmas."

"Riiiiight," K-pop said. "Because bucket lists are things you *want* to do before you die."

"Okay," I said. "Then whatever the *opposite* of a bucket list is."

101

"I get it," Linus said abruptly. "I'm not gonna make you do something you don't want to do, but we'll still need to figure out how to confront Christmas."

As the other agents whispered different ideas for plans to each other, I knew that the easiest way to get to Christmas was for me to go out there and talk to him myself.

The only thing about that was that every molecule in my body was against it, and I don't even know why! It wasn't that Christopher Moss was a terrible person to talk to! And it wasn't like I was some dark and brooding pre-teenager that kept to himself in public!

It was because I was one of the good guys, and he was one of the bad guys.

But is that even fair for me to say? I really don't know the kid, and didn't I just get done talking about how a villain had an origin where they *weren't* the villain?

Wasn't Vader a kid once too? Even the emperor was an innocent child at one time… no wait, that dude probably hatched from an egg, already *seething* with evil.

I looked back at Christmas and his goons. He was still just sitting at his table with the same Styrofoam cup he'd had all day, sipping it as if nothing else was happening in the world. There sat the one boy who I was afraid of – who I always had to turn away from because he saw me looking, and I knew what had to happen next.

"I'll do it," I said, turning back to my team.

Everyone stopped and looked at me.

"I'll go out there and talk to Christopher," I said, using his real name because it reminded me that he was just another sixth grader at Buchanan.

"Alright then," Linus said, nodding and *not* arguing with me.

Honestly, I knew that if *anyone* said it wasn't a good

idea, I would've changed my mind instantly.

"Then the only thing we have to do is figure out how to get you through the Suckerpunch agents," Maddie said. "Christmas might not have a problem talking to you, but his goons won't be too happy about it."

"So we take the goons out of the equation," K-pop said.

"And just how do you think we can do that?" Maddie asked. "Use the mall intercom to make an announcement that all Suckerpunch agents should check and see if they left their headlights on in the parking lot?"

"Ummm, no," K-pop said. "But are any of you thinking what I'm thinking?"

Janky's eyes lit up. "My bean balloon!"

K-pop shut down the idea immediately. "No again," she said.

Janky's shoulders slumped. "Okay then, first you tell me what *you're* thinking, and then I'll say *I* was thinking the same thing."

K-pop paused. "There's that one thing... that one thing you're good at..."

Janky scrunched his face, obviously thinking harder than he had all day. "What one thing?"

"You know," K-pop sighed. "That thing you're never allowed to do around me."

Janky kept thinking, but the answer wasn't coming.

Again, K-pop sighed as if she were disappointed in herself for having brought it up. "You can..." she paused, cringing. "...crop dust them."

Janky's eyebrows lifted so high that both of his entire pupils were out in the open, floating in the canvas of his white eyeballs. "No way!"

K-pop folded her arms, shut her eyes, and let out a long sigh. I think she already regretted mentioning it.

"Crop dust them?" I asked. "What's that mean?"

Janky was about to talk, but K-pop spoke first.

"Ah, ah, ah!" she said. "Let *me* explain because if you do, it'll just come out as a gross boy thing!"

"Right," Janky said, standing at attention.

Linus, Maddie, and I waited eagerly for K-pop to explain what "crop dusting" meant.

"Janky has this *talent*," K-pop said. "To basically let out a benchwarmer on command."

"Wait, wait, wait," Maddie said. "First, what's a benchwarmer?"

"You're not making this easy," K-pop said, pouting. "I'm talkin' about *farts*, people!"

"You call them *benchwarmers?*" I asked, holding back a laugh. "That's the best thing I've ever heard."

"Well, it's about to get better," K-pop said sarcastically. "So you know how crop dusting planes fly down a path in the field and let out pesticides and stuff?"

Linus and I looked at each other. Maddie covered her mouth like she was going to puke. I guess she figured out what K-pop was gonna say before she said it.

"So crop dusting is when someone walks down an aisle at school," K-pop said, pausing again because she obviously hated explaining it. "And then lets out an SBD. By the time anyone notices something off about the air, the guilty person has already left the aisle, leaving the kids in their seats arguing about which one of them did it."

Janky leaned over, smiling proudly. "Silent, but deadly."

"Thank you," K-pop said. "So that's what crop dusting means."

"So gross," Maddie whispered into her hand.

"I'm actually kind of impressed you can do that on command," Linus said.

"I think you mean 'concerned,'" K-pop said. She turned to Janky and nodded once, and with a hint of a smile on her face. Even though it was gross, she still thought it was funny. "Dust 'em, buster."

"Hang on to this for me," Janky said, handing me the red water balloon. "But don't use it."

I took the balloon. It was heavier than I would've imagined, and I could feel all the little beans inside. Seriously, one of the grossest things I've ever held. "I thought you made this so one of us *could* use it if we needed?"

"I did," he said. "But don't use it yet! Do you know how long it took me to make that? Have you ever tried filling a small water balloon with baked beans before? I woke up at four-o-clock this morning just to get started, and had to go through thirty balloons and *seven* cans of beans!"

"Seems like kind of a waste of beans actually," I said, holding back a smile.

With a smirk, Janky winked at me. "Now you know how I can summon an SBD on command."

And with that, the smile on my own face disappeared, replaced by a confused, grossed-out face. "*You ate seven cans of baked beans this morning?*"

"Before you were even awake, son!" Janky said proudly.

We all laughed, more nervously than we meant to. Janky was a cool dude, but he was definitely an odd one too.

Janky took a deep breath, puffed out his chest, and marched right out toward the Suckerpunch agents.

"I can't believe he can just do that," I said, watching as Janky walked away.

"The boy's got a lot of talents," K-pop said. "*Some* of them are actually useful too. In fact, I wish I could say *this* talent *wasn't* useful, but here we are using it."

Janky quickly made his way over to the Suckerpunch

agents at the tables surrounding Christopher Moss. He walked fast enough that the agents didn't notice him at first.

He slowed down when he was in the aisles between all the agents. It looked like he was staring into space. And then he started walking again, maneuvering through the agents.

Most of the kids in suits didn't even pay attention to Janky since he wasn't moving toward Christopher. A couple glanced at him through their sunglasses, but never did anything about it.

I'm not sure why, but for some reason I was expecting to see a green cloud or something. Maybe it's from all the years of watching cartoons.

Within fifteen seconds, Janky had cut a path through the Suckerpunch agents, and was already on his way down the mall.

The four of us in the hallway waited patiently, watching the faces of Suckerpunch agents.

"Maybe it didn't work," Linus whispered.

"Trust me," K-pop said. "Just give it another second or two."

But before she even finished her sentence, one of Christopher's agents scrunched his nose, leaning his head back like he was taking a huge whiff of something.

At that exact second, all the rest of Christopher's agents winced at the same time. Janky's air biscuit must've risen to nose level because they all noticed it together.

Many of the boys covered their faces with their hands, shouting about how they could hardly breath.

"What's that smell? What's happening?"

"Sick, man! What the heck is that?"

"OMG, it's in my mouth! That smell is in my mouth! I'm gonna hurl!"

Christopher set his drink down, but wasn't acting grossed out. In fact, it even looked like he was sniffing the air. But if he was, it didn't look like he could smell what Janky had been cooking in his bowels for the last eight hours.

Within thirty seconds, the kids in Suckerpunch had all left the tables surrounding Christopher. I guess protecting their leader wasn't as important as getting away from a nasty smell. A loyal bunch of goons indeed.

With Christopher by himself, I stepped forward to meet him, but K-pop grabbed my elbow.

"Wait another minute," she said. "I just want to make sure the ghost of Janky is gone before you go out there."

Christopher was now by himself, looking pretty annoyed that his agents had left him, but he never got up from his seat. He was just sliding his Styrofoam cup back and forth on the table.

From the hallway, I could hear all the noise from the food court down below as it filled with the sixth graders and teachers of Buchanan School.

Now that Christopher wasn't surrounded by kids in suits, I could see that there were three oversized shopping bags under the table he was at. He must've spent some money right after the buses got to the mall and dropped us all off.

I hated waiting because it meant my brain had time to convince me the whole thing was a bad idea. I was already on the edge about it, so it wouldn't have taken much to push me over.

"I can't wait," I said. "It's gotta be now or never."

"Okay," K-pop whispered.

"Good luck, dude," Linus said.

"We're right behind you, Brody," Maddie said. "You'll do good. Just talk to him, and nothing else. Don't let him suck you into an argument. Remember – this kid is a smooth talker."

"Gotcha. Just talk to him," I repeated, walking away from my three friends in the hallway.

My knees were shaking in my jeans as each step I took became harder than the last, and I was only halfway between the hallway and Christopher Moss.

He was still sliding his drink back and forth on the table, but now he was leaning his head on one of his hands. The annoyed look on his face had turned to boredom. With eyes glazed over, he stared into space like he was deep in thought.

Was I crazy? Was I about to make a huge mistake? Was there still time to turn around? Had he even noticed me yet? What was I even gonna say to him?

And then it hit me – I had no idea what I was going to say to Christopher Moss.

Too bad I was already standing in front of his table, and he was looking me right in the eye. I was expecting anger and hatred to spew from him, but instead, got just the opposite.

108

Christopher smiled with one side of his mouth as he sat up straight. "Brody!" he said as if we were old fishing buddies. He pointed at the chair in front of me. "Please, sit!"

"I'd rather not," I said, but after I realized my knees were still shaking, I changed my mind. I pulled out the metal chair. "Fine, but only because I want to. Not because you invited me."

Christopher's nostrils flared, but he didn't raise his voice. "Of course not, Brody. You do what you want."

I sat on the soft cushion of the metal chair and slid it forward, glancing at the shopping bags by Christopher's feet. Each bag had the same thing inside of it. I couldn't tell exactly what he had bought, but only that they were made out of the same dark blue thick canvas, and each had a bright orange logo tag sewn into the material.

I was almost instantly hit by the sudden strong smell of perfume. It smelled almost exactly the same as the perfume from the fountain.

Christopher's forehead wrinkled as he glanced at the empty seats around him. "It seems my agents had *better* things to do."

"I think they were grossed out by something," I said.

"By your friend's SBD, no doubt," Christopher said, shaking the ice in his Styrofoam cup, trying to get the last bit of soda to drop to the bottom.

I said nothing, shocked that Christopher knew what Janky had done.

"Come on," he gloated. "You think I don't know about crop dusting?"

"But why weren't you as grossed out?" I asked.

The leader of Suckerpunch lifted his cup and scraped his fingernails into the soft Styrofoam. "I love etching patterns into Styrofoam cups, don't you?"

The patterns on the cup had no rhyme or reason – they were just the doodles of a psychotic kid. "Sometimes," I said. "But that has nothing to do with why you weren't grossed out by Janky."

Christopher paused. "Set your phone on the table," he said coolly.

"What?" I asked.

"Set. Your. Phone. On. The. Table," Christopher repeated. "I don't need you secretly recording this conversation like some kind of *spy*. You're a smart guy; I know that. Keen as mustard, right? Now put your phone on the table."

As I pulled out my phone, I felt kind of dumb that I *hadn't* thought of that idea. Setting it on the table in front of him, I clicked the home button to show him that it was locked and *not* recording anything.

Christopher continued, pointing at his nose and taking a deep breath through it. "All I can smell is that blasted perfume.

110

I was... *near* the fountain when it happened. But that's why Janky's plan didn't bother me. Because I can't *smell* anything right now."

"Near the fountain," I said. "I have a source that says *you* were the one who poured the perfume into the fountain."

The leader of Suckerpunch took a sip from his drink, but ignored what I said. "I'm going to assume that you're here because you want to join my agency," he said confidently, in higher pitched voice as if he were singing the words. "And I'm here to welcome you with open arms, Brody. Of course *you* can join. You will have made... *all* my dreams come true by siding with me," he added, totally sarcastically.

"Thank you," I said. "But I'm doing just fine with Glitch."

"Glitch is in shambles," he snipped, leaning back in his chair. "Don't *act* like it's not, because I *know* better." Christopher's face tensed up as he hissed through his teeth. "I *knoooooow* better, Valentine. I know everything. You should've learned that by now."

I didn't say anything.

Then Christopher's attitude changed again, back into delightful, and almost instantly. It was creepy how quickly this kid went from angry to happy to pyscho. "Alright, fiiiine," he sang as he held his arms out. "Glitch hasn't been flushed just yet, but even *you* have to see that its time is coming. You and your friends? You're like expired bread waiting to get thrown out. Hardened mac and cheese that *nobody* wants to eat. You're the nasty clear juice that shoots out of a ketchup bottle if you don't shake it. Uhhg, or even worse, the clear juice from a *mustard* bottle!"

I watched as Christopher gagged at his own description.

He shuddered, and then snapped his head to the left, cracking his neck without using his hands, but never taking his eyes of me. Flippin' creepy!

Christopher continued. "It doesn't surprise me that you're here, you know. You're so into whatever Glitch is doing that I knew it was just a matter of time before you put on your big boy pants and marched over to confront me about something you have no idea about. After all, you're a hero now, aren't you?"

"No," I said, not sure if that was supposed to be a burn or not.

"How's Linus holding up?" Christopher asked smugly.

"He's fine," I said.

"And Maddie? The two of you an item yet or what?"

"No," I said, embarrassed. "I mean… that's not… it's none of your business."

"Alright," he said. "But I can tell from your voice that you're not *against* the idea."

I hated that this kid was reading me like an open book.

Christopher leaned his head to the side. He was looking at Linus, K-pop, and Maddie, waiting in the hallway behind me. "And again, they've sent you out here *alone*."

"I *chose* to come out here alone."

"Did you though? Did you really? I mean, you seem to be on your own a lot during these kinds of missions. It's sort of like Glitch *knows* you'll do *whatever* they ask of you because you just want *so* badly to be part of their little group!"

I could feel my face getting hotter as Christmas spoke.

I also realized my brain had gone back to calling him "*Christmas*," and not "*Christopher*."

"There was a young man named Brody," he said, bobbing his head up and down at me. "Who didn't have one single homie. So he joined up with Glitch, but then he got ditched, and now he's just one great big phony."

Yeaaaaaah, talking to Christmas might've been a

mistake.

Christmas pointed at the red balloon in my hand. "What's with that thing?"

"Nothing," I said.

The leader of Suckerpunch looked at me with sad eyes. "Aw, dude! I didn't mean to get ya right in the feels!"

Maddie had warned me of this – that Christmas had a way with words, and she was right. This kid sitting across from me was something different from anyone I'd ever met. It was like his brain was geared specifically to be an evildoer.

"Hey," Christmas said softly, like he was speaking to a sobbing five-year-old that just fell off their bike. "Chin up, buddy. I know we've had our differences, but let's put those aside, huh? What do ya say? Wanna join Suckerpunch? I'll waive all your membership fees, except for the cost of the t-shirt. You gotta pay for that still. Because I'm not making a profit off those shirts, it's outta my hands."

I couldn't listen to it anymore, and opened my mouth without caring about what I said. "We know you put Regina up to the text message game!"

Christmas put his hand over his heart and gasped. "What? I would *never* do such a thing to such an innocent—" he coughed out a laugh. "Yeah, alright, ya got me."

I blinked, in shock that Christmas didn't even try to deny it. "But…" I said, stuttering. "But why'd you do it?"

The boy across the table from me cleared his throat and glanced around to see if anyone else was listening. "Let's just say I'm getting a hefty payment out of it."

"Not anymore," I said, surprised at how strong my voice sounded even though I felt weak. "You're toast. We got you this time. Regina is a witness, and I guarantee she'll let Principal Davis hear the whole thing after we've gone to him."

"Brody!" Christmas said, smirking. "Where's this 'big

boy' attitude coming from all of a sudden? You sound like the kind of kid who thinks they're in control!"

I was going to defend myself, but Christmas switched gears into "pyscho" mode again.

Slapping the table hard, the crack echoed through the mall, and without trying to cover up for it, he screamed at me. "*But you're not in control! Are you?*"

An electric chill shot through my body like a bolt of lightning as I flinched away from the insane boy.

"You've got *nothing* on me," Christmas said, disgusted. "You're just a *dog* chasing after cars! You think you've cracked the case on this bad boy, but you haven't even scratched the surface!"

"What are you talking about?" I said.

"Your whole world is controlled by something else," Christmas said. "You think Cob was giving out the orders? You think Linus has a clue about what he's doing? You guys are getting strung along like puppets by the real kids in charge."

I remembered Cob had talked about the "powers that be." That must've been what Christmas was talking about.

Exhaling slowly, Christmas turned the volume down on his voice as a sly smile returned to his face. "There's no bridge connecting Regina and me. There's nothing there except for her word, and what good is that when *she* was the one sending you all those texts. But you wanna know the kicker? You want me to crack an egg of knowledge over your head?"

I didn't answer.

Christmas wiggled his fingers in the air, and then sang "*Spoiler alert!* Regina's the one who asked *me* for help. It's not the other way around this time." He pounded the butt of his fist against the table. "Man! I hate *ruining* surprises!"

My heart stopped. I patted my chest with my open palm

114

to get it going again. Okay, not really, but that's what it felt like.

Christmas could see the confusion on my face and he continued to floor me with his words. "I'm sure by now you've noticed the show choir has been absorbed with the set they've been creating all afternoon. It's quite elaborate, and everyone in the show choir is required to help, but... has Regina been helping at all? Has she been sweating away, moving huge boxes back and forth with the other kids in the show choir?"

I paused. "No. She's been running around the mall taking selfies. But... her parents were here. They came to watch her performance."

Christmas snapped his fingers at me. "Connect those dots, Valentine..."

"But if Regina's *not* in the show choir, then her parents can only be here because they *think* she's in it," I said, staring at the table. "But why would she lie to them?"

"Cha-ching!" Christmas was giving me a hint. "Don't forget that membership is $200 a month!"

"*That's* why Regina seems to have so much money all the time," I said. "She faked being a member of show choir to keep the money for herself. But... why the selfie game? Why send us all over the mall?"

"Because I told her to," Christmas chuckled. "Yeah, that was all me. She came to me, asking for help to cancel the entire trip, which I actually tried to do earlier."

Little light bulbs were switching on in my head. "That's what the sign was for this morning." And then I remembered the girl who shouted. "That was Regina in the cafeteria! She tried to start a food fight so the school would cancel the show before we even boarded the buses!"

"Didn't work," Christmas said. "I knew it wouldn't, but that didn't stop her. She came to me again at the mall and asked for my help, so I did. I told her exactly what to do, and she did it perfectly, distracting you like the bugs you are."

"Distracting us?" I asked.

Christmas turned around. "She's planning on sabotaging the show choir performance. If they don't perform, then her parents will never learn that she's *not* in the club."

I stood from the table, pushing my chair out with the back of my legs. I could see the crowd gathered in the food court down below. All the sixth graders were there, along with the parents of the kids in the show.

Behind the stage, near the vat of gazpacho, were the students in the show choir. They were wearing thick purple robes and waiting just out of sight from the crowd.

I blinked, swallowing hard. I could feel my brain wanting to panic as it made me open my mouth, grasping at whatever straws it could find. "I could make a scene – shout at all the adults over the railing and get the teachers up here along with mall security. Once they're standing over us, all I'd have to do is start shouting things about how you and Regina are in cahoots. Sure, I'll look like the crazy kid, but I know Regina will break down in a second, giving you up."

Christmas sighed, glancing at his watch. "You won't do that," he said.

"No?" I asked. "What makes you think that?"

"Because you have no time to do it," Christmas said. "You'll be too busy saving those kids in the choir who happen to be taking the stage even as we speak. Trust me, Regina's got something amazing planned for the show, and if you wait here, you'll definitely have balcony seats to the greatest show Buchanan School has ever seen."

"Why?" I asked. "Why are you telling me all this?"

"Chaos," Christmas answered, without emotion. "Chaos doesn't choose sides. I helped Regina and messed with you guys all day. Now I'm helping you and messing with her. In the end, I'm the only one who comes out on top. That, and it's pretty funny. As the good guy, you're predictable. I know you'll try to fix whatever I do, so the path you've chosen is limited by the choices that *I* make. But I'm over here, doing what *I* want. This is the best game I've ever played, Brody, and I don't think I'll stop anytime soon."

I looked over the edge of the railing. Christmas wasn't lying – the kids who were waiting to take the stage had already gotten on top of it. Whatever Regina was going to do would likely happen before the show started, which meant I only had about a minute to get down to the first floor.

I sat there, faced with a choice. Christopher Moss was a clever kid, and if I walked away from him, he'd for sure get away. But the kids in the show choir were in for a show that wasn't part of their concert. Regina was somewhere down below, about to unleash whatever prank she had been planning.

I bit the inside of my cheek, because I knew what I had to do.

I had to leave Christmas and help those kids in the show choir.

Pushing my chair out from under me, I started sprinting

through the shoppers on the second floor, carefully cradling Janky's water balloon in my hands. There wasn't even time to tell Maddie and Linus what was going on, so hopefully they'd just follow my lead.

I scanned the crowd over the railing as I ran to the escalators. Regina's parents were taking their seats right in the front row. Her dad had his cell phone out, taking a picture of her mom who, right before the flash, made a duckface of her own.

So that's where Regina got it.

The mall security guards were *still* at the escalators watching the kid who was *still* walking in place between the first and second floor.

"Just shut the escalator off!" I said as I slowed down at the staircase next to the mall security guards.

One of the guards scratched the back of his head. "Huh," he grunted. "Why didn't we think of that?"

As I marched down the steps to the second floor, I heard the buzzing of an alarm, and then the sound of gears slowing down. The boy on the escalator started moving toward the second floor as soon as the steps came to a stop.

At the bottom of the staircase, I hung a left and continued to run.

"Slow down!" one of the security guards hollered.

The thick crowd of mall shoppers forced me to obey the guard's command. Everyone was beginning to gather outside the food court for the show choir concert.

People were pretty much shoulder to shoulder as the crowd swayed back and forth like an ocean of humans. Waves of adults moved swashed this way and that, taking steps at the same time to try and keep the whole machine moving together without falling.

Pushing my way through the crowd, I felt like I was at a

rock concert trying to get to the front of the stage because I wanted the best seat in the house. The reality was *kind* of similar though – I was trying to get to the stage of a concert, but because I needed to try and save the day instead of hoping to get a guitar pick or something.

I was getting frustrated at the traffic jam. It was like these people weren't even trying to move! Time was running out, and I knew it. My stomach was turning over as my palms started sweating. If I wanted to save the show choir, I had to do more than I was doing so I did what any normal kid would do when they wanted to get past a bunch of adults.

Rolling the bottom of my shirt around the water balloon, I dropped to my hands and knees and crawled through the legs of everyone in my way.

"Outta the way, people!" I shouted.

I was able to make progress. A few adults moved their feet, jumping back like an animal had just brushed up against them. The balloon was bouncing around in my shirt. If I was thinking with a clear head, I would've tossed the balloon in a trashcan, but I wasn't so I didn't.

At the edge of the crowd, I popped out on the floor and pushed myself to my feet. The food court was *filled* with people that were waiting for the show to start. I wasn't surprised since the Buchanan School show choir *did* win the city championships.

It was a pretty big deal, but it was also in danger.

I narrowed my eyes, scanning the crowd for Regina. Her parents were up front taking pictures of everything with their cell phones. Other parents were seated behind them, laughing and talking as they waited for the choir to start singing.

The sixth grade students were scattered around the food court, sitting at tables with their friends, while teachers hovered over them making sure everyone was accounted for as they checked names off clipboards.

I looked up to see if Christmas was still watching from above, but he wasn't there anymore.

"Brody!" Maddie barked as she suddenly appeared by my side, catching her breath. "What's your deal? Why'd you take off like that?"

Still searching the food court, I spoke. "Regina's planning on sabotaging the show choir concert. I have to stop her before she can do it!"

"Why would she do that?" Maddie asked. "Why would she mess with her own show?"

"Because she's *not* in the show choir," I answered.

Maddie was smart. She was able to instantly connect the dots that Christmas had to help me with. "That's why she was so awkward around her parents! I knew there was something off about that whole thing!"

"Right," I said. "And now we have to stop her before she does whatever she's planning on doing."

The kids in the show choir were waiting on the stage as the show choir teacher took his spot in front of them. A whole line of kids were at the side of the stage in their costumes too, which meant there was still time before the performance.

All the students in the show choir were wearing the same thick purple robes with the hoods up, covering their faces. They stood tall, holding their hands together in front of them. It looked like the Grim Reaper's family reunion.

"There!" Maddie said, grabbing the back of my arm with one hand, and pointing toward the kids in line with her other hand. "She's wearing one of the robes!"

Maddie ran down the side of the food court. I did my best to follow, but she was fast, probably one of the fastest kids in school. It took every muscle in my body working together to even *kind of* keep up with her, but I still lost her when she disappeared through a wall of people.

I clutched at the cramp in my side. Seriously, as much running as I did, how come my body still wasn't used to it?

Pushing through all the people, I searched the group of kids wearing robes. There was a hole at the middle of the line where a few students looked upset, as if something bad had just happened in that spot.

Behind the students, I saw two people picking themselves up off the ground, both with purple robes draped over their faces.

Right then, a few kids cut me off, pushing me aside to walk past me. They were dressed in black overalls and had huge duffel bags slung over their shoulders. Whatever they were carrying sure looked heavy. Three more kids marched by, wearing the same overalls and bags.

The bags were made of dark blue canvas and had a bright orange logo sewn into the material. I wouldn't have thought anything of it, except that they reeked of perfume.

"Hey," I said, but then got cut off a second time by someone who jumped in front of me. It was Jake, but without

121

his wolf pack.

"Gotcha," he said. "And this time, Chase isn't around to save you."

Jake was a whole world of trouble that I didn't have time for, so I said nothing and moved to the side of him. But he wasn't about to let me go anywhere. He had a chip on his shoulder that he needed to brush off.

"C'mon, man!" I said.

With both his hands, he shoved me backward, pushing my shoulders like he wanted a fight.

Of course, I wasn't going to give it to him, but I didn't know what to do. Everyone around me was watching this kid pick on me, but nobody was saying anything.

If we were at school, a teacher would've jumped in before anything happened, but we weren't at school. We were at the mall, and all the teachers were far away at the back of the food court.

Jake stepped up again, pushing against my shoulders. I could feel the baked bean balloon roll out from my shirt. I threw my hands out catching it before it fell to the floor.

"I'm sorry about the sign!" I said. "But you gotta believe me when I say I *had* to wear it!"

"Oh, you *had* to?" Jake asked, shoving me a third time. "Why did you *have* to?"

I knew his fist was going to come my way any second.

"You wouldn't understand!" I said honestly, trying to keep the balloon from falling out of my hands.

Jake pulled his fist back, and my body tensed up.

But before he could throw his punch, someone else stepped between us. He caught Jake's fist with his shoulder, but the kid was so big that Jake's punch just rolled off his side.

It was Edgar, and he didn't look too happy.

Jake stumbled, regaining his balance and glared at the huge kid in front of him.

Standing in front of each other, it was clear that Edgar was twice Jake's size. He could've easily crushed Jake, but he didn't. In fact, he didn't move forward at all. Edgar simply held out his finger and wagged it at Jake like he was scolding a child.

Jake also noticed the size difference, and without his wolf pack behind him, he wasn't acting as strong as he had on the bus.

I could tell Jake wanted to say more, but was ruffled by Edgar's size. "Whatever, man," he said, looking at me. "You aren't worth the trouble."

Edgar had saved me from Jake.

He turned his head just enough to see me, and then nodded. "Vampires are real, bro."

I LOL'd. "Vampires," I said, returning the nod.

Edgar rubbed his shoulder as he walked away. He didn't say anything else, but he didn't have to.

I slipped past the other students in the show choir, to where Maddie and Regina had fallen. The line of show choir kids was enough to block out the view of the rest of the crowd in the food court.

We were at the spot at the very front of the food court, where the vat of gazpacho sat. The woman handing out the samples wasn't around anymore, but the vat was still filled with ice-cold vegetable soup.

"Maddie?" I asked.

Both kids popped up and stared at me. They both looked like a hot mess of blonde hair and purple robes.

"Um," I said, and then asked again, "Maddie?"

Both girls answered at the same time. "*Yeah?*"

Uh-oh.

There were two of them. I was staring at *two* different Maddies.

"Took you long enough," the Maddie on the right said. "Now help me take Regina to the principal."

The Maddie on the left replied right away. "Yeah, help me take Regina to the principal, Brody!"

I blinked, feeling like my brain had just short-circuited. I knew Regina looked a lot like Maddie, but I never thought it would be impossible to tell them apart if they were standing next to each other. Even their *voices* sounded the same! The real Maddie was gonna kill me later for not being able to see the difference.

The other students behind me watched carefully as the strange situation unfolded in front of them.

"Whoa," I heard someone say. "Those two could be twins."

"Right?" I said over my shoulder.

So there I was... standing in a group of kids wearing purple robes, carefully cradling a water balloon filled with onion baked beans in my hands, and staring at two different Maddies.

"Earth to Brody!" the Maddie on the right said, super annoyed. "Get your head back in the game!"

"Yeah, dude!" the *other* Maddie said. "Quit spacing out!"

I couldn't stop looking back and forth between the two identical blonde haired girls, who only had slight differences between them, like one of them had a small mole on her cheekbone and the other didn't, but I had no idea if the real Maddie had a mole there or not!

If the whole thing wasn't so bananas, all three of us probably would've joked about it.

Regina had been wearing a purple robe, but it must've gotten tangled when Maddie caught her. I'm not sure exactly what happened, but in their short scuffle, Regina's robe had gotten wrapped up over her shoulders and ripped in two because both girls had sheets of purple fabric hanging from their necks.

"Get on with it, Brody!" Maddie on the right commanded. "Time's running out! Those kids are gonna start singing any second now, and if we don't take Regina to Principal Davis, those kids are completely flooped!"

"I know!" my voice cracked, making it obvious that I had no clue who was who.

"Soak her with the beans already!" the Maddie on the right continued.

Ah, only the real Maddie would know the balloon was filled with beans.

The Maddie on the left made a face so angry that it

scared me. "Don't you dare do it! Soak *her* with that balloon filled with beans!" she said, nodding her head at the other girl.

Nevermind what I just said since both Maddies said something about the beans.

"I swear to the ghost of James Buchanan himself," Maddie on the right said, "If you pitch that balloon of beans at me, you'll regret it for the *rest* of your life."

That kind of sounded like my Maddie.

"Ditto!" the Maddie on the left said.

Ugh...

"Will the real Maddie please step forward?" I asked, half-jokingly.

Both of the girls took one step forward, and they both had the exact same "*annoyed-to-play-this-game*" look on their faces.

I lifted the baked bean balloon, darting my eyes between both of the blonde girls standing in front of me.

All the kids behind me gasped, waiting for me to make my move.

"I'm the real Maddie!" the Maddie on the left said with a tremble. It almost sounded like she was going to start crying. "Brody, listen to me. It's *me, your* Maddie. Remember all the good times we've had? Remember all the funny things we've said to each other?"

"OMG," the Maddie on the right said. "Seriously, Brody, I'm the real Maddie and this is seriously starting to get on my nerves! The fact that you can't tell us apart is a little disappointing!"

Finally, I had an idea. I looked at the Maddie on the right, who was clearly more upset of the two girls. "If you're the real Maddie, then tell me – what was the first thing you said to me when we met?"

The girl clenched her firsts as her face turned red. "Like

I can even remember something like that!" she said through her teeth, and then she turned the question around on me. "What did *you* say to *me* when we first met?"

I sighed, nodding. "Touché."

The Maddie on the left took another step toward me. Her eyes twinkled with what looked like tears. "Brody," she said again, softly. "Please... please don't do this. Don't make a mistake. Okay? We've come so far as friends... please... do the right thing."

"The right thing?" Maddie on the right asked. "You mean by popping that balloon on *me?*"

The Maddie on the left didn't look away from my eyes. She took another step in my direction, reaching her hand out like she wanted me to take it.

I wanted to back up, but the kids behind me kept me from moving in that direction.

"Please," the Maddie closest to me pleaded again, her eyes twinkling. "Give me that baked bean balloon."

And then, as if the planet screeched to a stop, I knew exactly what I had to do. It was so obvious that I almost felt like an idiot...

Holding the water balloon out at the two Maddies to keep them at a distance, I reached into my front pocket, pulling out my cell phone super fast because I needed to catch both versions of Maddie off guard.

As I raised it in front of me, I unlocked it. "Say cheese!" I said, snapping a picture.

The instant the camera flashed, the Maddie on the left leaned her head over and made a duckface. The Maddie on the right kept the angry look on her face like a statue.

And just like that, everyone knew who the real Maddie was.

Regina tore her purple robe off her head and dropped it

on the floor. She stumbled backward, and then started running when she gained her balance.

I squeezed Janky's water balloon in my hand. Maybe his little invention was going to be useful after all.

Pulling my arm all the way back, I lifted one of my legs like I was about to pitch a baseball. My eyes were focused on Regina as she ran through the other kids in the show choir line.

I jerked my whole body forward, hoping to throw the water balloon like a professional, um, water balloon thrower?

But the beans inside the balloon, sloshed around, making the thing hard to grip. Without thinking, I squeezed the balloon tightly in my fingers so I wouldn't drop it.

And then...

...the whole stinkin' thing popped right in front of my face.

Janky wasn't kidding when he said he filled it with onion-baked beans, like I didn't believe him or something, right?

My hair, face, and the front side of my body fell victim to the disgusting invention that Janky had spent the dark hours of the morning carefully crafting.

Beans dripped off my arms as I stood there shocked, like a toddler after they accidentally spilled milk all over themselves.

Maddie snorted a huge laugh.

The kids behind me jumped, surprised at the fact that *water* wasn't in the water balloon.

As I whipped my hands to get the bean juice off my fingers, I couldn't help but laugh. It was so gross, and so stinky, but I could see how it was super funny.

I was actually relieved that it popped over me and not Regina. I wasn't thinking when I was about to throw it, so in way, it saved me the trouble I would've gotten in if she *was* the one who got soaked.

It was a happy accident.

Maddie turned, looking for Regina who had, *again*, disappeared. "Do you see her?"

I wiped some of the juice away from my eyes. "I can't see much of anything," I joked.

"She couldn't have gotten far," Maddie said. "There are too many people here for her to cause such a scene. She has to be close."

"In case we don't catch her," I said. "I'm sorry. It's my fault that she was able to escape."

"It's nobody's fault," Maddie said, still searching the area with her eyes. "I mean, if you would've known who was who back there, it *probably* would've helped. And if you hadn't burst that balloon all over you, that would've helped

130

too."

"I know," I said. "I should've been faster back there. I should've done things different."

"Stop saying that," Maddie said. "You did what you did. There's no right or wrong about it. We just have to find Regina now. We can talk about all that afterward."

"You're right," I said. "I'm just sorry. I really hope we *can* find her, but if we don't, then I'm sorry. I just... I just hope we can still be friends if all this fails."

Maddie stopped searching and looked at me. "What're you talking about?"

"I mean," I paused. "If Regina gets away with all this, then I can't see Glitch carrying on much longer. And if Glitch falls apart, then, y'know, I understand if you're angry with me. You've been so cool to me for the past few months, and I just wanted to say that I'm sorry if all this is for nothing."

"What are you trying to say?" Maddie asked.

131

After another short pause, I spoke. "I'm just... I've been afraid of losing you as a friend if Glitch falls apart."

Maddie came toward me with an angry look on her face. I couldn't tell if she was annoyed or concerned. "Brody, you're talking like a crazy kid," she said. "Why do you think I want Linus to a good leader?"

I shrugged my shoulders, not sure about what Linus had to do with it.

"If Linus is the leader," Maddie explained, "then that means you and I will be on more missions together. I *want* to be out here with you, Brody. There's no way we won't be friends, even if this all fails."

"Wait," I said, confused. "You used a double negative, I think. So are you saying we *will* be friends or we *won't* be friends if Glitch falls apart?"

Maddie rolled her eyes, and then slugged me in the chest. "You know what I meant, now spot being such a sap, and let's find Regina!"

I smiled like a dork.

"Uhg!" Maddie said.

I stared into the crowd of people waiting for the show choir to do their thing. Regina couldn't have gotten far with how many people were now gathered in the food court.

Plus her plan was to somehow sabotage the performance, which pretty much guaranteed she was somewhere nearby.

I looked again at the remaining kids in purple robes as they marched onto the stage. Regina had taken her robe off so I knew she wasn't up there with them anymore.

And I knew she wouldn't have risked being seen by her parents by hiding in the food court, or even standing with the crowd around us.

I glanced over at the vat of gazpacho that was behind the stage.

And then I saw it. The tuft of blonde hair peeking out from the side of the vat.

But the instant I noticed it was the exact same instant the vat started to slowly tip toward the show choir students on the stage.

OMG. Regina was going to dump the vat of cold vegetable soup on the ground, spilling it into the food court. I had to hand it to her. If there was anything that would stop a performance, it'd be a tidal wave of vegetable soup.

With no time to think, I jumped at the vat of gazpacho, grabbing the opening at the top, trying to stop it from tipping.

"Brody!" Maddie said from behind me.

"The vat!" I said. "Regina's tipping it!"

"It's too late!" Regina shouted like a madwoman. "It's too heavy and it's already going over!"

I tightened my grip on the huge tub of soup, trying as hard as I could to pull it back, but Regina was right. The whole thing was already tipping. Even with Maddie's help, the thing was impossible to stop.

"Brody, what do we do?" Maddie groaned.

Regina moved back, dusting her hands off. She had gotten the massive vat to tip, and all she had to do was watch as her plan succeeded.

The crowd around us finally realized what was happening and gasped together as they watched the vat tip farther and farther in slow motion. Too bad none of them thought to help the two kids trying to keep it from spilling!

My palms were starting to hurt, cramping up as I pulled harder on the vat. It was going over, and there was nothing I could do to stop it, short of jumping into it!

Wait... did I just? Yep. In that fraction of a second, I

had an idea.

I let go of the side of the vat, took a step back, and dove into the vegetable soup, face first.

Maddie screamed as I grabbed onto her forearms and she grabbed onto mine, pulling me back toward her, using the weight of my body to get the vat of gazpacho to level out.

All the show choir kids on the stage screamed too as they turned to look at us.

In fact, practically the entire mall was looking at us. I would've been embarrassed if it weren't for the fact that Maddie was right by my side outside the vat of gazpacho.

Teachers and parents of some of the kids in show choir began to gather around us. They were packing in so tight that Regina couldn't slip away. She just stood there, staring at us with folded arms.

The show choir teacher was the first to say anything.

"You oughta be ashamed of yourself!" he said angrily. "All these people have come here to see the show choir, and you're back here pulling pranks! How immature! How very immature!"

"Yeah!" Regina added from the side.

"But—" I started to say as my body sloshed around in the soup.

"No!" the choir teacher shouted. "Wait until Principal Davis gets here. I promise you'll be suspended, no, *expelled* from Buchanan!"

"Yeah!" Regina said again.

I wanted to say something, but Regina's parents showed up.

"You *wrecked* our daughter's performance!" Regina's mom shouted as she stormed toward Maddie and me. "My baby has worked so hard and we paid a *lot* of money for her to be part of this show choir!"

The choir teacher spoke again. "That's right! All these

parents are here to see how hard their children have worked for—" he stopped. "Wait, Regina? Who's Regina?"

"Our daughter!" Regina's mom cried out. "The *star* of the show! The one with all the solos!"

"Solos?" the choir teacher said. "*Nobody* has a solo in my show... and there's no one named '*Regina*' in my class either."

Maddie leaned closer to the vat of gazpacho. "She even told her parents she had a solo?"

"More than one apparently," I replied.

"Of course I'm in the show choir," Regina said desperately, chuckling from the side. Her eyes were wide open like she was flabbergasted at how the choir teacher could forget such an important member of the show choir. "It's me!"

The show choir teacher turned his head, super confused. "I have no idea *who* you are."

Regina's parents both stared at her. She stared back. The smile on her face slowly faded out as her eyes watered.

Finally, Regina broke down completely, sobbing. "I'm not in the show choir! I was never in the show choir! I just lied about it so I could keep the money you thought you were paying for me to be in that class!"

My jaw dropped as I slumped my arms over the side of the massive vat I was still stewing in. Y'know, the taste of gazpacho was starting to grow on me.

Principal Davis eventually showed up and helped me out of the gazpacho bath. Thank goodness too because my toes were starting to go numb.

After giving me a towel, he let me sit at one of the empty tables on the side of the food court.

Regina was taken to one of the tables behind me to explain to her parents and Principal Davis what she had been doing all day. I overheard her entire confession. She opened with the text messages back at the cafeteria, and closed with me jumping into the vat and saving the day.

Maddie was at the table with me too, making fun of how much I stunk of vegetable soup, but how it was still better than the smell of onion baked beans.

From the front of the food court, the show choir had taken its place back on the bleachers and had started the show.

After the terrible day I had just gone through, it felt good to know that everything was still moving forward, almost as if nothing had even happened. That's the true purpose of Glitch – to keep the weird things behind the curtain so the rest of the world can still go on normally for everyone else.

After a few minutes, Principal Davis led Regina back to the table we were sitting at. Her parents were still in the hallway, arguing with each other.

"Regina has something to say to you the two of you," Principal Davis said to Maddie and me. Then he looked at Regina. "When you're done here, you can join your parents. We'll have a meeting about this on Monday before school."

Regina's cheeks tightened a smile.

After Principal Davis left, Regina stared at the table and spoke. "I'm sorry," she softly murmured.

"I forgive you?" I replied. "Is that what I'm supposed to say?"

"No, seriously," Regina said, looking up at me. "This whole thing was stupid. And it was because I made a stupid decision months ago to *not* join the show choir. It's all my fault, and I've been caught. And honestly, it kind of feels good to not have to carry this lie around anymore."

I sighed, looking at Maddie. She shrugged her shoulders.

"You didn't get away with it," I said, raising my eyebrows. "I'm drenched, but everyone else is fine. Even the show choir's performance is still going on."

Regina nodded. "Right," she said.

"So what's gonna happen to you?" Maddie asked.

"Detention," Regina said.

"Seriously?" I asked. "That's it?"

The way Regina smiled showed that she was surprised by her punishment too. "Right? Principal Davis said that if the vat had actually tipped, then there would've been a more severe punishment, but since you saved the day, all I get is a week's worth of after-school-detention. Plus it's *'strike-one'* for their *'three-strikes-you're-out'* policy, but that's okay because I don't plan on getting another two strikes."

I was happy to hear that Regina learned her lesson so quickly.

Regina continued. "It's kind of funny," she said to me. "You saved the day, but also saved me from getting in much worse trouble, so not only do I have to apologize, I guess I want to *thank* you for that too."

I pulled a chunk of tomato out of my hair. "Don't mention it," I said.

Regina and Maddie laughed.

"There's just one thing I want to know," I said.

"Yeah?" Regina said as she folded her hands on the table in front of her.

"Why Christopher Moss?" I asked. "Why'd you seek *his* help in the first place? Like, what made you want to *pay* him?"

"Pay him?" Regina repeated, confused. "I didn't pay that creep anything. And I didn't seek *him* out. He was waiting by my locker this morning with the whole 'cafeteria sign' plan for me to see."

"Whaaaaaaat?" I whispered.

"I was already freaking out about the show today because I knew my parents were going to be there," Regina said, "but I didn't know what I was gonna do about it.

Christopher told me his idea before school, and then said that if I didn't go along with his plan, *he'd* tell my parents himself."

"But since you were already worried about your parents finding out," Maddie said, understanding. "You just went along with his plan because it was gonna help you anyways."

"Exactly," Regina said. "And it was supposed to end at school with a food fight, but didn't. When I got to the mall, Christopher was here with another plan for me to dump the gazpacho over. And again, I went along with it because it would've kept my parents from learning the truth about me, and didn't involved hurting anyone… at least physically."

As Regina kept talking, my mind went back to Christmas, and what he had said to me outside The Pretzel Palace.

Why would he tell me Regina was paying him a hefty sum? What were his exact words?

"I'm getting a hefty payment out of it," I whispered.

"Huh?" Maddie asked.

"That's what Christmas told me," I said to Maddie.

"Who's Christmas?" Regina asked.

But I ignored the question. "He never actually said Regina was paying him," I said, thinking aloud. "He just said he was getting a hefty payment… but what does that…"

The shopping bags that Christmas had under the table appeared in my mind. The ones filled with dark blue canvas material and a bright orange logo sewn into the top. It was the same one that the three kids in jump suits were lugging around with them earlier, just before Jake cornered me. The kids that stunk of… perfume.

"Jake had pushed me around right after those kids bumped into me," I said. "If he didn't distract me, I would've put two and two together right there!"

"What're you talking about?" Maddie asked, worried that I sounded like a crazy person.

As I spoke, the words came faster and faster out of my mouth. "Those kids were lugging around bags filled with something. They stunk of perfume which means that they had just been around the closed down fountain!"

My mind just about exploded.

"That whole section of the mall is shut down and closed off!" I said, sitting up straight in my chair. "Those kids! Those kids were carrying silver dollars in those duffels bags!"

I shot up from the table and ran through the mall again. Maddie was right behind me, but Regina didn't get up.

Five minutes later, I was back in the closed off part of the mall as the rest of Glitch trailed behind me, running through the stink of perfume, toward the Silver Dollar Fountain.

The lights from under the water continued to shine. The gold reflection of the tiles at the bottom of the fountain danced on the surface of the water, but the silver reflection of the silver dollars wasn't there anymore.

I sat on the edge of the fountain, staring at the bottom of the empty pool.

Maddie stood silently over me. I never explained what I was talking about as we ran to the fountain, but she knew.

The rest of Glitch stood a few feet behind us, shocked.

Linus gripped the top of his hair like he was stressed. "Of course," he sighed.

Maddie pointed to the side of the fountain. "Brody," she said. "Look."

The thing that Maddie was pointing at was an empty Styrofoam cup with patterns etched into the side. It was the same cup that Christmas had with him all afternoon.

"It was Christmas," Maddie said. "He left it here because he knew we'd find it."

"He did it again," I sighed. "He played us again. This was his plan the entire time. Not Regina. Not the gazpacho. Not the show choir. This. Stealing all the silver dollars."

"He got away with all this money," Maddie said. "There must've been hundreds of silver dollars in this thing."

Janky gasped. "That dude's rich," he said. "And a thief. A smart, rich, thief."

Linus looked like his eyeballs were going to pop out of his head. I think it was too much for him to handle.

Maddie took the spot next to me. "Is this it? Are we done then? Is Glitch over?"

I gulped, feeling the last bit of hope disappear from me.

"Are you guys for real?" K-pop said loudly. "Like, you're all joking right now, right?"

141

We all looked at K-pop, confused.

She walked over to one of the silver dollar machines next to the fountain and slipped in a dollar bill. Almost immediately, a coin dropped to the metal cup at the bottom with a "CLINK" sound.

"Look at the face of the coin!" K-pop said, more frustrated than angry. She was holding the coin out for us to see.

We all leaned over to get a better look.

On the front of the silver dollar was the face of a gorilla. The same gorilla that was on the sign out in front of the mall.

"These aren't real silver dollars," K-pop said. "They're fake ones, custom printed for this fountain. They collect all these coins at the end of every week and put them back in the machines for people to buy all over again. Christmas didn't get away with anything! I'm not surprised that he didn't notice the gorilla since none of you guys did either!"

"So he's just lugging around worthless coins right now?" Linus asked, breathing a sigh of relief.

"He's got three bags full of those things!" I said. "I saw his goons carrying them!"

"Then that's three bags full of fake coins that he's not going to know what to do with," Maddie laughed.

I hunched over, resting my elbows on my knees as I snickered to myself. The day I had just gone through was easily one of the worst days I've had as a secret agent, and it was only by good luck that it had turned out the way it did.

The show choir was at the other end of the mall performing their award winning show. Regina had been stopped just in the nick of time, and even though my clothes were ruined by cold soup, I didn't care because I knew I was the only one who got nailed by her plan.

And Christmas was somewhere out there, opening a bag full of coins that were worthless. I just wished I could see the look on his face when he realized it was a gorilla on the coin and not a president.

Linus, K-pop, and Janky were walking ahead of Maddie and me, back toward the food court at the center of the mall.

Maddie and I were quietly walking with each other when my phone buzzed in my pocket. At first, I was worried that it was going to be another text telling us to take a selfie somewhere else, but then reminded myself that Regina was done with that.

I brought my phone out, and read the message from the unknown number on the screen.

Agent Valentine,
Christopher Moss has gone too far this time.
Suckerpunch needs to be stopped. Stand by for our orders.
- The Powers That Be

I stared at the screen, reading the message over and over until my brain finally caught up with my eyes.

"What's that?" Maddie asked, curious.

I smiled. "I think we just got our next case."

Stories – what an incredible way to open one's mind to a fantastic world of adventure. It's my hope that this story has inspired you in some way, lighting a fire that maybe you didn't know you had. Keep that flame burning no matter what. It represents your sense of adventure and creativity, and that's something nobody can take from you. Thanks for reading! If you enjoyed this book, I ask that you help spread the word by sharing it or leaving an honest review!

- Marcus
m@MarcusEmerson.com

AND DON'T FORGET TO CHECK OUT
TOTES SWEET HERO!

TOTES SWEET HERO ALSO
INCLUDES THE BONUS SHORT COMIC
diary of a 6th grade ninja STINK BUG SABOTAGE

Marcus Emerson is the author of several highly imaginative children's books including the 6th Grade Ninja series, Secret Agent 6th Grader, Lunchroom Wars, and Totes Sweet Hero. His goal is to create children's books that are engaging, funny, and inspirational for kids of all ages - even the adults who secretly never grew up.

Marcus Emerson is currently having the time of his life with his beautiful wife and their four amazing children. He still dreams of becoming an astronaut someday and walking on Mars.

Made in the USA
Lexington, KY
17 November 2016